SEA CHANGE

MAGIC & MECHANICALS BOOK 2

JESSICA MARTING

SHADOW PRESS

Sea Change (Magic & Mechanicals #2)

Copyright © 2021 J.L. Turner

ISBN 978-1-989780-09-1

Cover art by German Creative

CHAPTER 1

5 September 1887

*D*ear Mr. Quinn,
  It is with great exasperation that I must remind you of your impending deadline for your new book. As we are accustomed to your maintaining contact during your writing process, and we have not heard a word from you regarding your current work in months, we are greatly concerned about your progress, or lack thereof.

  Your latest deadline has been extended. We expect to see a completed manuscript no later than 1 November. Please also take note that if this new pattern of behavior continues, Cardwell Press will be forced to terminate their working relationship with you.

  Sincerely,
  Peter Renton
  Lead Editor, Cardwell Press

THE CARRIAGE JOLTED TOO much for Lucien Quinn's liking.

This is what happens when one spends too much time in the city. One grew used to the comforts of steam cabs on paved roads, among other amenities.

Amenities he was voluntarily giving up, all for the sake of an adventure novel he was contractually obligated to write. If he made any more missteps or delays, his career would vanish. It was vital that he finish this book and turn it in, preferably before his publisher's deadline of the first of November.

There are no steam cabs where I'm headed. No paved roads. At least there will be electricity.

A particularly hard jolt nearly had his head crashing into the carriage's ceiling. The driver slapped the roof from his perch outside, undoubtedly a weak attempt at an apology.

He was doing this for the change of scenery. He'd rented the estate through a leasing office for its remote location, for being as far away from the bustle of London as Lucien could get without leaving the country. Lucien had repeatedly demonstrated over the last eighteen months that he was incapable of writing in the city any longer. His renting the estate to write in was his last-ditch effort at saving his writing career.

And my sanity. If he could finish this book and turn it in and possibly start another, he might be able to get his life back in order.

Another hard jolt had him knocking around the carriage's interior, forcing him to smother a yelp of irritation. He gritted his teeth, looked for something to hold on to, and came up short. *Damnation.*

Lucien was forced to grip the edge of the leather seat, worn through in spots, and hope for the best. *At least if I'm suffering from a head injury, I'll have a worthy excuse for not turning in my books.*

The carriage lurched to a halt. Lucien heard a muffled curse, and thumps sounded through the carriage as the driver jumped down from his perch.

Lucien, having rarely left London since he was a boy, was unfamiliar with this part of England and had no idea how long a carriage journey would take between the Manchester airfield and Greaves Estate on the coast. But when the carriage door didn't open and the driver didn't announce their destination after a couple of minutes, he grew worried. Even though the last thing he wanted to do right now was speak to another person, he let himself out of the carriage to see what had just happened.

Rain lightly misted the air, which was more humid than Lucien expected for early September in this part of the country. He found the driver hunched over one of the back wheels, quietly cursing to himself. "Is there anything I can help with?" Lucien asked.

The driver started. "No, sir. Just a bent wheel. The road's hard here, and I just want to make sure this beast will take us right to where you need to go."

"Does the wheel need to be replaced? I can help with that."

The driver rose to his feet and brushed off his trousers with his gloved hands. "No, sir. The wheel's well enough to see us there. I can replace it once I leave you to it."

"It's dangerous to travel with a damaged wheel," Lucien protested. "I'm not worried for myself so much as you."

"No need for that. Wheels bend all the time."

"All right," Lucien said. "Now I'm worried for both of us."

The driver surprised him when he burst out with a laugh. "Don't be worried for both of us, just yourself.

You're the one headed to a cursed castle. I'll just be traveling slower than usual."

As if the weather conspired to make the driver's words a little more sinister, the rain increased, and a rumble of thunder sounded nearby. "What do you mean, 'cursed'?"

If he'd thought the driver would hem and haw about rumors he'd heard, Lucien was mistaken. "Greaves Estate is a, what you toffs would call a 'comedy of errors,' I suppose."

Lucien didn't quite consider himself a toff, nor would he refer to a house in those terms, but he nodded and waited for the driver to continue.

"Greaves died," the driver said. "He built it for his wife, catered to her every whim, built some strange things in that house. She died before he did. Then he lost his mind and made the house even crazier. It's a bit of a legend around these parts."

Lucien already had a basic grasp of the circumstances of the estate's construction, including the demise of its original owners. "I learned about them when I signed the lease."

The driver shrugged. "No one stays there that long. Even the owner doesn't want to live there."

"I'm sure it's much more profitable to rent it out to blocked writers like me." The rain was falling harder still now, and the thunder boomed more closely.

"I recognized your name from the dirigible manifest when I went to the airfield," the driver said. "My wife's quite the fan. So am I, to be honest."

Shame washed over Lucien, the feeling as tangible as the rain sliding over him.

He flashed back to striding off the dirigible's rampway at the Manchester airfield, waiting impatiently for the carriage driver he'd ordered to take him the rest of the way to the estate. He'd found the driver—this man—jovial and accommodating, hauling his trunk in the back of the carriage like it weighed nothing. And Lucien couldn't even be bothered to ask him his name.

He found his voice. "Thank you. And I apologize for not asking earlier. What may I call you?"

"Just John, Mr. Quinn." He held out his hand.

Lucien didn't hesitate to shake it. "Please, call me Lucien."

John withdrew his hand. "Well, Lucien, the sky's about to open up and piss all over us. Get back in the carriage. We'll be at the estate soon enough."

It was dark when the carriage reached the estate after a slow and careful drive. The rain had let up at least, which Lucien appreciated.

He could hear the sea crashing against waves when he alighted from the carriage but couldn't see it from his vantage point. No matter; he would have plenty of time to explore the sea when it was daylight.

But you aren't here to meander along the beach. You're here to write. There was that annoying voice reminding him of his true purpose at this place. He would have no chance nor excuse to explore the estate until he had some work completed. His remote location aside, Cardwell Press and his editor there had ways to establish contact with him and monitor his progress. Lucien absolutely did not want to risk his editor's ire any more than he already had. Peter Renton had been patient with his last two adventure novels being turned in late, but his grace had worn dangerously thin in recent months.

A suited man emerged from the estate's massive front

doors and strode confidently to where the carriage was waiting. When he got closer, Lucien could see the man was older than he looked from a distance, with a face as lined as a map. But he was fit and stood upright, shoulders back, and when he said, "Mr. Quinn," even John straightened in respect.

Lucien held out his hand. "You must be the caretaker." He had exchanged a few telegrams with the man when he secured the estate's lease.

"Edwin Hammond, yes," he replied. "You're late."

"Yes," said Lucien, although he had no idea what the time actually was. "My apologies. There was a problem with a carriage wheel on the journey here. Will it be all right if the carriage driver finds a spot on the property to repair it before he leaves?"

"No need for that," John said quickly. He looked up at the house and quickly turned away as if he'd just spotted a ghost in a window. "The old girl will make it back into town just fine."

"What town?" asked Lucien. "There's nothing around for miles."

"There's a village about two miles east," Edwin Hammond replied. To John, he said, "You will find an inn there that can help you. The staff will replace your wheel while you enjoy a hot meal."

"Thanking Mr. Quinn for his offer, but I'm going to take my carriage to the village," John said. "Begging your pardon, Mr. Hammond, but this place doesn't sit right with me."

Lucien thought the driver might have actually shivered when he looked back at the house.

And to the driver's credit, the estate was a little unsettling. Even in the dark, Lucien could make out strange, sharp turrets on the roof that resembled the pointed ends of spears. Stone gargoyles, their faces contorted in agony, were installed between the windows on all three floors and flanked either side of the front door. The gardens were bare of anything but grass rapidly turning brown at the approaching winter and the property's trees already wrapped in burlap.

If a ghost was ever going to haunt a house, this would be the perfect place to do so.

"Mr. Quinn," said Hammond.

Lucien tore his gaze away from the house. "Yes?"

"Your driver and I will bring in your luggage," he said. "Then both of us will depart."

That came as a surprise to Lucien. "But you said you're the caretaker?"

Hammond nodded. "I don't live on the property. I live in the village. I will stop by twice a week during your stay to check on the property, per your lease terms with the owner."

"Is there any staff living on-site?"

"None." Hammond regarded him curiously. "You were informed of this when you rented the estate, were you not?"

Lucien may have been told those details, but damned if he could remember them. His mind had been little better than Swiss cheese over the last couple of years, full of holes and missing substance. "Mr. Greaves himself might have mentioned that in a telegram, yes," he mumbled. He'd received a single telegram from the owner after he signed the lease, a long, rambling thing that Lucien only glanced over.

"Mr. Greaves has always been a conscientious host," said Hammond sternly. "He may not live in his ancestral home, but he ensures those who rent it are aware of its limitations. Now, a cook does stop by twice a week to replenish the pantry and leave foods that can be enjoyed cold, and the kitchen does have clockwork appliances that even a bachelor will find easy to use."

"I'm not a bachelor," said Lucien before he could stop himself. "I'm a widower."

Hammond was silent for a moment. Lucien immediately regretted his words. There was no need to embarrass the estate's caretaker and, in a way, his lifeline.

Finally, Hammond said, "My condolences, Mr. Quinn." To John, he said, "Let's see about bringing Mr. Quinn's belongings into the house."

ONCE HIS TRUNK was installed in the bedchamber Lucien was assigned for his stay, John was turned away, and Lucien led on a tour of the house, courtesy of Hammond.

Much of the home's decorating scheme matched that of the exterior. There weren't any glowering gargoyles to be found inside, but it was still maudlin as if the house was in mourning. The wallpaper was stained black in places from wall-mounted sconces, now empty of torches. Some rooms had been outfitted with electric appliances; in others, there wasn't so much as a candle available.

But the lack of lighting was hardly the strangest element of the house. Hammond gamely pointed out which doors led to nowhere, which corridors ended in dead ends, and provided a hand-drawn map of the places in the house that Lucien would actually need to access during his stay. "The first Mr. Greaves was an eccentric man," Hammond said more than once. "That eccentricity has been passed down. His great-great-nephew, the man who owns the estate, certainly embraces his own eccentricity. Why, he and his daughter live on a dirigible, sailing across Asia and Europe, never staying anywhere for long."

"I only need a change of scenery," Lucien said as they walked through a parlor on the main floor. Floor-to-ceiling bookshelves filled the space, along with a sideboard stocked with liquor and a massive rolltop desk. He stopped in his tracks when he saw the desk. "What room is this? It isn't as gloomy as the rest of the house." Now that he'd stopped, he could take in the flower-printed wallpaper and green damask curtains pulled shut against the window. Shadow boxes of butterflies and pressed flowers were arranged on the only wall not covered by a bookcase.

"This was the first Mrs. Greaves's morning room," replied Hammond. "The current Mr. Greaves informed me you're a writer."

"Yes."

"I suggest you use this room to write in," said Hammond. "When the weather is good, the sunshine is bright enough in here, and it's routinely aired out by the staff between tenants. Now, let me show you the rest of the house."

Lucien nodded politely as Hammond continued the tour, unable to stop thinking about the room that was supposed to be his study.

It was exactly the sort of room Emmaline would have found charming. She hadn't been as squeamish about things like pinned insects the way he was. She had been fascinated by those sorts of morbid curiosities: butterfly collections, taxidermied animals, hair mourning brooches. She never encountered a *memento mori* she wasn't interested in.

He pinched the bridge of his nose between two fingers,

willing away thoughts of his late wife. Then he felt guilty for doing that.

"Mr. Quinn?"

Hammond had an uncanny knack for noticing that Lucien's mind had wandered off. "Yes?"

"Are you particular about water?"

Lucien had the impression that Hammond had asked him that question while he was woolgathering. "It's the essence of life, so I suppose I am."

That answer drew a small smile from the caretaker. "Mr. Greaves intended for this home to be a showpiece," he said. "He wanted to have as many marvels of engineering to his name as possible, so he ordered the construction of an underwater ballroom. Unfortunately, that was as much as he could accomplish before his health declined after his wife passed away. Consumption." He shook his head. "According to legend, he was never the same after it took her."

"I think a single feat of engineering to his name is remarkable."

"As do I, but he wanted more of them. Let me show you."

They walked down a long corridor, the plush carpeting muffling their footsteps. Hammond opened a door inlaid with an enameled design of blue waves at the end, then flipped switches on a board mounted inside the doorway. Lights clicked on, illuminating a stairway, and he gestured for Lucien to descend. The briny scent of seawater filled Lucien's nostrils, and a wave of uncertainty crashed over him.

What kind of madman builds a room below sea level?

Just as quickly, he silently answered himself. *A madman wanted to see if we could travel by air and made it happen. I have no fear of flying in a dirigible.*

But apparently, he had a fear of water, or at least a subterranean ballroom constructed decades prior.

When Lucien didn't move, Hammond smiled again. But this one was more forced than the last. "Follow me," he said. "I assure you it's perfectly safe."

Swallowing his anxiety about the whole matter, Lucien obeyed and followed the caretaker down the stairs. A dark red runner shot through with golden embroidered seashells, immaculately maintained, ran down the center of the winding spiral staircase.

He was a bit dizzy when they reached the foot of the stairs, and it took him a few seconds to regain his bearings. When he did, he nearly staggered back from surprise.

He hadn't been able to conceive of what an underwater room might look like. The electric lamps throwing yellow light across the room highlighted the swirling dark water outside its high glass walls and highlighted the well-polished dance floor. A small orchestra pit in the corner held chairs and brass music stands, waiting for musicians who would never arrive. Other than that, the place was devoid of furniture.

But Lucien didn't care about that. He was standing in a subterranean ballroom. How many people in England could claim they had done such a thing?

Amusement crossed Hammond's face as he took in Lucien's reaction. "When the tide goes out, you can see above the waterline," the caretaker explained. "At any given time, this room is anywhere from nine to twenty feet below sea level."

Lucien wasn't overly familiar with how tides worked, so he merely nodded in agreement. "This is stunning."

"It truly is. If the current owner wasn't so attached to his dirigible, he might spend more time here just for this room alone. Shall I show you the bowling lane next and then the boathouse?"

But Lucien barely heard Hammond's words. He slowly paced around the ballroom, occasionally looking at the water outside.

He might have found a solution to his dilemma of writing in the room that Emmaline would have loved.

This place would be his study while he lived at Greaves Estate.

Hammond was still waiting for an answer. Lucien didn't care a whit about a bowling lane or greenhouse, but he still said, "Please, lead the way."

CALLA WASN'T sure exactly how long she'd been swimming, but the daylight that broke through the water's surface was long gone, or what little daylight she'd seen. She could feel a storm brewing on the surface, not one with enough volatility to take down a ship, but dry land was certainly experiencing a downpour.

The water was only a little less choppy this far below the surface, and it was far darker than she'd ever seen it. Or perhaps it was her panic, her fear of being chased and caught again, that made everything look more sinister than usual.

Tears formed in her eyes, and she let the water wash them away as she swam, unsure of which direction she was headed in, only knowing she had to escape.

Was I successful? Will he find me here? Am I going to be caught in a net again and dragged through the water back to his laboratory?

Lights beckoned in the distance, golden and welcoming. Calla froze in place, shocked by the sight. "No," she said aloud. Speaking made little bubbles float away from her, up to the water's surface. "That shouldn't be possible."

For a couple of seconds, she wondered if she'd finally gone mad. Human lights visible in the sea's depths weren't sights seen, well, *ever*.

She slowed down a little, cautious that it might be a trap. Calla's sense of direction was no longer as finely honed as other mermaids, but it was still better than the average human's. She knew she hadn't swum in circles for hours following her escape. Plus, her captor hadn't had an underwater laboratory, complete with electric lights at his disposal, just a warehouse on a grimy dock.

And the lights had to be electric. Their glows were too uniform, too perfect to be anything but.

Even if the lights weren't connected to her captor, who knew who possessed them. Sane people didn't build underwater rooms.

Her captor had called her room an "observatory." Like she was a specimen instead of a living being. A shudder rippled through her.

She swam slowly, careful not to attract attention to herself. There were only a few pieces of kelp and long algae strings to act as camouflage, neither of which was especially helpful. So she pressed her belly to the silty seabed, hair swirling around her. She hoped it just looked like a sea plant.

She slid along her front to the lights and saw she was looking into a room.

It was almost empty of furnishings, save for a small area with a cluster of chairs. Its floor shone under the electric lightbulbs, looking slippery in the light. But there were no instruments of torture, no angry human men glowering at her and demanding she bend to their will.

When Calla closed her eyes and concentrated, she

couldn't sense any human-originated vibrations in the water, from the strange subterranean room or otherwise.

She'd made it. She really escaped.

Exhaustion pulled at her, and with it, the need to rest. This place was as good as any.

And in a few hours, she would keep moving.

CHAPTER 2

*A*s far as Lucien could see, Hammond was an efficient caretaker, but dear *God*, the man simply didn't want to leave.

The estate was large enough, which would account for the amount of time Hammond spent taking Lucien through it, but he also acted as historian. By the end of the tour, Lucien knew everything about the estate's original owner and his obsessive love for his late wife, and his quirks that resulted in things like the subterranean ballroom. And while Lucien appreciated the caretaker's passion for the property, he also just wanted to sit down, pour a stiff drink, and have a light, cold supper before trying to get a few words on the page before bed. It was already approaching eleven in the evening.

It wasn't until Lucien gently suggested to Hammond that it might be time for him to head back home to the village before the weather got worse that the caretaker agreed to leave. Turning over a large ring of keys to Lucien, Hammond left via the front doors, and Lucien was grateful to lock the door behind him.

He'd spent the day traveling and, therefore, with more people than he was used to. *I'm getting to be a rather crotchety man in my old age, aren't I?*

Could thirty-one be considered old age? He'd been contemplating that since his birthday a few weeks prior.

Was twenty-seven considered old age? That was how old Emmaline was…

No. Not thinking about her right now. He wasn't thinking about her or the morning room she would have loved. No, Lucien was avoiding that room, except to fortify himself with the contents of one of the bottles there, and he was going to try to write in the subterranean ballroom.

He could sit in a study anywhere in England and wait for inspiration to strike. When would he get another chance to write in a room under the sea?

He traced his steps back to the kitchen and, after seeing what was left for him by the estate's cook, fixed a plate for supper. He noted the modern variety of clockwork implements that his own kitchen lacked in his London townhouse and he had no use for here. The place had a working icebox, a kettle, and a stove. He didn't need anything else.

He ate his meal of cold roast beef, sandwiched between two slices of bread, and then headed to the bedroom Hammond designated as his during his tenancy for his pencils and foolscap. Then, steeling himself, he went to the study he was thinking of as Emmaline's room. Electricity had been installed in this part of the estate, a feature he was grateful for as he poured a generous amount of whiskey into a glass. Pencil case and paper tucked under his arm and glass in hand, he walked through the house to the subterranean ballroom.

He'd made a note that most of the places Hammond

gave him permission to wander had electricity, and he would respect that as much as he wanted to explore. He tamped down that compulsion, knowing it was only his procrastination that was keeping him curious, as he set up a makeshift desk in the ballroom's orchestra pit. He arranged his supplies on a brass music stand and balanced his whiskey glass on the empty seat next to him.

He leaned back and took in the room, a smile on his face.

For the first time in a very long time, he felt somewhat at peace, watching the waves angrily swirl against the high glass walls.

He left his paper and pencils on the stand and, glass in hand, paced around the room.

Just to look. I'm not procrastinating at all.

All right, he *was* procrastinating. But he was just getting used to a new space, of the kind that likely didn't exist anywhere else.

Had any balls actually been held here before the Greaves family passed away? He'd have to ask Hammond the next time the caretaker stopped by the estate. Although Lucien was sure Hammond would give him a detailed rundown of every person and tenant who had ever inhabited this place, along with a chronological list of every party that had ever been held since the manor's construction.

Lucien sighed. He was curious but not curious enough to listen to the caretaker's stories.

I'm simultaneously deathly lonely, and I cannot abide the presence of other people.

How he hated feeling that contradiction.

"I wonder what this looks like during the day," he murmured to himself as he wandered the length of the room. He touched the glass wall: cold, impenetrable. "I hope to God it stays impenetrable," he muttered and finished off what remained in his glass.

The whiskey left him feeling comfortable. Not quite drunk, but he hadn't had much to drink since Emmaline's funeral for the sake of his own health. Drinking away his grief and regret would only prolong the mourning process by way of making him forget about his troubles when he wanted to confront them head-on.

He walked another few feet to the opposite end of the ballroom from the orchestra pit and stared out at the dark water. Its waves roiled a little more against the glass than it did earlier, and a crack of thunder sounded. The storm that started on his journey to Greaves Estate was picking up speed.

Dark tendrils floating in the water, reaching for the surface, caught his attention, and he crouched down to look at them a little better. Lucien would've thought it was nothing more than kelp strings, but kelp, to his knowledge, wasn't so fine and hair-like.

"What the hell?" he said, voice bouncing off the ballroom's glass walls.

He was looking at human hair. A head was pressed face down into the seabed's silt.

Lucien thought he might be sick. He rose to his feet on shaky legs and looked frantically around the ballroom for a more portable light source. None of the electric sconces on the walls could be removed.

The orchestra pit! He'd spotted a box of candles waiting on a music stand. He bolted to the opposite side of the room and found the candles, a mix of old-fashioned wax tapers, and the new, modern flameless models. As Lucien didn't have a set of matches nor a tinderbox on him, he picked out the first flameless candle he could find and twisted its tiny brass switch until it flickered on. It wasn't as bright as a regular candle, but it would have to do.

He rushed back to the spot where he'd seen the body and held up the flameless candle to the glass. He desperately hoped that what he'd seen was nothing more than a trick of the light, or perhaps he was drunker than he thought and conjuring up delusions.

His heart sank. That was definitely a body. He could make out bare shoulders with the added illumination, and the long dark hair he'd initially spotted ebbed and flowed against them in the water.

"Oh, Christ," he said aloud. "There's a dead woman outside the ballroom."

How did he go about getting her out? Would Edwin Hammond know what to do?

As he said the words, the dead woman shifted position. At first, Lucien thought her movement was the result of the storm, but she raised her head, blinked, and stared straight at him and his flameless candle. Her full lips formed a perfect "O" of surprise, and then her eyes met his.

Lucien stumbled back on his hands, nearly falling over. An undignified shout escaped him.

And then, gallantry.

"I'll be right there to save you!" he yelled at the glass. "Just... just give me a moment."

The last thing he saw before he bolted up the stairs was her face contorted in confusion.

LUCIEN TORE through the house to the servants' entrance off the kitchen. Hammond had pointed out that it led to the greenhouse and boathouse on his tour, and the boathouse was where he needed to get to. It was close enough to where he guessed he'd seen the trapped woman, and he could row his way to her location. Perhaps luck would be on his side, and he would find a deep-sea diving suit in the boathouse. It would be strange if the estate didn't have at least one, he thought.

He tore through the back garden, heedless of the rain soaking him, the mud squishing through his shoes, until he reached the boathouse. Mercifully, Hammond had included a key to the structure in the giant ring he'd left behind, and Lucien was able to read the label for it thanks to lightning flashes.

He threw open the door and surveyed the boathouse's contents.

There was nothing nautical in there save a pair of tiny boats and pairs of oars mounted on wall hooks and the diving suit Lucien guessed would be there. One look at the suit told him there was no way he could possibly learn to use it in the short amount of time he had to save the woman. "A boat it is," he said and marched forward to the nearest one. He flipped some wet hair out of his eyes and pulled it and the oars off the wall.

A peal of thunder sounded, loud enough that Lucien thought the boathouse shook. He looked at the boathouse's empty slip and considered launching from there, but he didn't have a key to open the locked door that led to the sea.

Hesitation at the stupidity of his near-future actions had him frozen in place for a second. *Move, you idiot. Someone is dying!*

Bracing himself, he bolted back into the rain and kept

running until he reached the strip of beach belonging to the estate. He could see the lights of the subterranean ballroom glowing nearby, so he put the boat in the wildly choppy water, pushed it out, and jumped in, heedless of the seawater soaking his shoes and trouser cuffs.

That was easier than I thought it would be.

His elation at launching his boat was short-lived until he tried to row toward the ballroom. He realized then that he didn't have a clue as to how he would get the woman out of the water. He hadn't noticed any life vests or rope in the boathouse, and as he flopped the oars on the water, trying to get in the direction where the water glowed from the ballroom's lights, he considered that he might have made a mistake.

A wave, larger than the others he'd seen so far, crested toward him, towering over his head.

Lucien's life didn't flash before his eyes when he hit the water and struggled to reach the surface. All he could think of was the poor woman struggling on the seabed, how cold she must be, how he had failed to save her.

SHE HAD MADE A MASSIVE MISTAKE.

Regret and fear coursed through Calla as she swam through the increasingly aggressive waves, looking for the man foolish enough to attempt a boat trip during a gods-damned storm.

It was her fault he was in this position, too: lured by lights and extremely fatigued, she'd set up a makeshift hiding spot in full view of a human man's underwater room. His hand-held light flashing in her eyes, coupled with the vibrations his voice sent through the glass walls and to her spot on the seabed to rouse her, had her alert.

What kind of idiot builds such a place?

She broke the water's surface and looked around for an idiot in a boat.

No, not an idiot. Someone kind who was putting himself in extreme danger to save what he thought was a drowning woman.

She spotted him almost immediately. He was in a flimsy, open-topped boat, of all the stupid things to be in during a storm, and flailing around in circles. "Where are you?" he shouted into the wind.

Calla's heart sank. The man's accent sounded English.

She hadn't made it as far away from her captor as she thought.

But before she could contemplate that further, a wave taller than the man was sitting in the boat knocked him from his seat.

Oh, hells.

Calla couldn't let him drown. She may still be in England, and he was an Englishman, but he wasn't connected to the man who'd held her for so long. He wouldn't have tried something so foolhardy if he was, and he would have recognized her as a mermaid, besides.

Calla dove back under the water, and with every sense on high alert, swam in his direction.

It wasn't especially deep in this part of the sea, but it *was* storming, and he didn't know how to swim. She knew that as soon as she zoned in on him, flailing and panicking, water getting into his lungs.

She wrapped her arms around him, and with the help of the water's buoyancy, rushed to the surface. He'd already stopped struggling against her, which was alarming. How quickly could humans drown, anyway?

"You absolute numpty," she yelled over the sound of

rushing water. "Isn't that your countrymen's preferred insult?"

A peal of lightning, worryingly close to their spot in the water, was her only response to her question.

"You fucking idiot!" she screamed in the wind.

Once again, he didn't respond to that, *her* preferred insult.

She stopped for a second to adjust his weight against her back, draping his arms over her shoulders. He was definitely more solid than she initially thought.

She frantically swam for shore and was out of breath when she reached the pebbly excuse for a beach. There wasn't much of a beach there since the tide was in, and she didn't want to chance leaving him there and risking his being swept back to sea.

That meant she was going to have to shift and find somewhere on dry land to leave him be.

"Fuck." Her favorite epithet was swallowed by the wind.

She hated shifting. Her captor had seen to that.

But she pulled him a little further away from the water, into mud that squelched underneath his body, and concentrated.

Her arms ached from hauling him through the water. Her back hurt. And the pain was only going to get worse as she shifted.

A crack of thunder shook the ground beneath them and swallowed her scream. She lay back against the mud with her mystery human, still not having awoken, and cried.

She didn't even know if he was still alive, and in that instant, she couldn't bring herself to care. Pain shuddered in her back to her lower body as it split and rent itself in two. A scream escaped her when she looked down and crackling lightning highlighted two legs instead of her tail and fins.

To the prone man, she sobbed, "You had better live through this, you son of a bitch."

She wiped rain and tears from her eyes and pressed her ear to the man's chest. She could pick out a heartbeat.

But he wasn't waking up.

Frustrated, Calla turned him on his side and leaned over, smacking him on the back as hard as she could. He coughed and spit seawater on the ground but didn't open his eyes or acknowledge her. In fact, it looked like he went right back to sleep, an oddly peaceful look on his face. His sand-colored hair was plastered against his forehead and ears, framing a face that was more youthful than she expected, perhaps about her own age of around twenty-seven.

"Gods damn it," she said.

She couldn't leave him here. Who knew how bad the storm would get? How long would it go on?

Her gaze darted around the beach. Behind her, a huge house stretched up to the stormy skies, the pointed roofs of its towers almost threatening. But there weren't any humans about, which was most important. No one had seen her shift, and no one would see a naked woman stumble around on her nearly useless legs.

He was so much heavier on land. She gave up trying to carry him and, grabbing his hands, dragged him toward the house on his back.

~

EVERYTHING HURT.

At first, Lucien thought he might be dead, and part of him welcomed his demise. There would be no more guilt, no more books to write. No more angry telegrams and letters from his publisher.

He quickly suspected, as he struggled to open his eyes, that death wouldn't hurt so much as he did right now. And Emmaline might be there to greet him.

As it was, he felt tremendous pressure in his chest and throat. He turned on his side and coughed and felt himself expel water through his mouth. "What the devil?" he said between coughs.

He was lying on a tiled floor, and the light was too dim to see clearly. When he blinked a few times, the lighting marginally improved, as did his blurry vision.

He tried to gain his bearings: he recognized the floor he was on as belonging to the kitchen, adjacent to the servants' door at Greaves Estate. How he ended up on the floor was still a mystery.

He was soaked to the skin, he reeked of seawater, and he shivered with cold. *What the hell happened?*

It came rushing back to him: the woman he'd thought had drowned. His running out into the night, during a thunderstorm, to save her. His humiliating grasp on boating and falling into the water. And then... nothing.

"You're awake."

He started and coughed again. The voice was unfamiliar, female, and he couldn't place her accent. He tried to sit up, but the motion hurt his ribs too much. He tried again and succeeded this time.

The first thing he noticed was the filth streaking his clothes, the second was how cold he was, the third was he was wrapped in a tablecloth. He couldn't remember the last time he'd been this cold. His teeth began to chatter.

Gingerly, he turned his head to look at the voice's source. When he saw her, he nearly fell over again.

She sat in a chair pulled away from the servants' table,

her long, dark hair dripping water on the tiles. Big, dark eyes watched him, shining in the dim illumination offered by a single electric light above the servants' door. Her full lips were downturned in a frown of—disappointment? Anger? Lucien couldn't tell.

But what he could tell was she was naked. Her breasts were covered by her long hair, and she had another table-cloth in her lap, but he could see she was naked, plain as day.

"You're awake," she repeated.

"I—yes, it would appear so." Lucien's voice was scratchy, and his throat felt raw. "Please forgive me. I'm a bit confused as to what's happened this evening."

"You're an imbecile," she said.

If she was expecting an argument from him to the contrary, she was going to be disappointed. "You're not wrong on that count," he said. Holding his breath against possible pain, he forced himself to his feet. He stumbled for the table and pulled out a chair opposite her, and sat down in it with a wet squish of fabric against wood. "I do kindly ask for some more clarification from you as to *why* I'm an imbecile in this particular instance." He wrapped the tablecloth around himself a little tighter.

She blinked in surprise. "You're alive after doing some-thing stupid," she said. "My help is no longer needed. If you'll excuse me, I must be on my way."

She stood up and wrapped the tablecloth around her body, and on shaking legs, started walking for the door.

"Wait," said Lucien.

He hoped she would. He didn't have the energy to go after her otherwise.

Gripping the brass doorknob for support, she craned her head over her shoulder to look at him.

"I saw you on the seabed floor," he said slowly. The

memory was returning to him in full color. "I know I did. You were drowning."

"Not at all. I was swimming."

"You were face down on the bottom of the sea," he said. "I even fetched a candle to ensure it. I thought you were in trouble."

"I wasn't in the slightest," she said. "I'm an excellent swimmer. And now that I see you haven't drowned, I will leave you to your own devices." She inclined her head to him, her hair sending a couple of water droplets to the floor. "Good night, sir."

"Don't go," said Lucien. He found enough strength to reach for her wrist, which she immediately pulled away.

"Don't!" she hissed.

Lucien obeyed. "My apologies. Please stay for another few moments," he pleaded. "You can't go back out in the storm like that."

He realized almost as soon as he said the words how ridiculous they sounded. This wasn't a woman afraid of the bad weather or the sea. Hell, she wasn't even wearing *clothes*!

"I can, and I will," she said. Her expression softened a little. "I truly cannot stay."

"Can you stay long enough just to tell me what happened?"

"I already did," she said. Irritation crept into her voice. "You mistook my night swim for an emergency and stupidly tried to rescue me. Instead, your boat capsized, and I had to save you. That's all that happened."

"Please forgive me," Lucien said. "But I'm not familiar with people who swim at night during storms. That strikes me as rather foolish."

"It's common where I'm from," she said curtly. "Now, if you please, I need to leave."

"Are you in trouble?" he asked suddenly.

That made the most sense: no one would be doing what she was if something terrible wasn't happening. Either she was in danger, or she had gone mad, and no matter the reason, she likely needed help.

Something shifted in her expression. It was subtle, but Lucien picked it up. Her lips turned further down just a little, and she blinked a couple of times like she was fighting back tears. Her shoulders slumped.

"I may be able to help you," he offered.

Her hand dropped from the doorknob, and he thought he might have convinced her. But when her eyes met his, he saw only sadness and fear there. "I have to leave England," she said curtly. "Can you help me leave England?"

"How the hell were you planning on leaving England by swimming?" he asked, incredulous.

"As I said, I'm a very strong swimmer," she explained. An edge had crept into her voice, and he suspected she was getting close to losing her temper. "I was hoping to reach Scotland as soon as possible."

"You could take a dirigible from Manchester…"

"I'd prefer to swim," she said, voice terse.

Lucien jumped in his seat at her tone but didn't argue.

She tried again. "Look, Mister…"

"Quinn. Lucien Quinn."

More often than not, when people learned his name, they spoke about his books. Either how much they enjoyed them or how they were looking forward to reading them. Lucien always smiled politely and thanked them for their interest, real or feigned.

But there was no flicker of recognition in her eyes. "I bid you good night, Mr. Quinn," she said. "And for your future safety, if you see people sleeping outside your strange underwater room, leave them be. Or at least ensure they're truly dead."

"You do realize that when people are at the bottom of the sea, they're usually dead?"

"No, Mr. Quinn. They are not. Dead people usually float after a time."

Lucien couldn't believe the argument he was getting into with this woman, nor could he believe that he was losing that argument. Usually, a naked person who had been swimming in the sea during a storm would be grateful for a chance to get a hot meal, a bath, perhaps a stiff drink to help them process everything that happened.

At least that's what Lucien would want. It was what he *did* want, although not in that order. A drink was definitely the first thing on that list. He tightened his grip on the tablecloth, trying to get warm. Perhaps he should change his clothes first.

"You saved my life," he said, trying another tack. "Is there any way I can express my thanks while still convincing you to set out when the storm is over?" His mind worked frantically, trying to think of ways to incentivize her to stay with him just a little longer. "I could pay for a ship or train ticket if you would prefer to avoid a dirigible. Anywhere in Britain or continental Europe, if you like." He held out his hands, which he saw were streaked with dried mud in the kitchen light. "I can't afford a ticket beyond those borders, I'm afraid."

Her back straightened, and he thought he'd convinced her. "Anywhere?"

He nodded. "Think of it as a thank you. I don't have a great deal to live for at the moment, but falling into the water may have changed that a little."

The words were a lie. He still didn't have much to live

for, but if it would keep her from barreling back into the water, he didn't have a problem telling her falsehoods.

She didn't look convinced of that. But Lucien knew it was the promise to pay her passage away from England that would keep her on dry land another day or two.

She sighed and tucked a wet lock of hair behind her ear. "All right," she said. "I will stay the night until the storm has passed. Then, you will buy a ticket to Scotland for me."

He nodded. "Of course."

"I'll stay here." She looked around the kitchen. "Will that be all right with you?"

"There are bedrooms upstairs," he began, but she waved him away.

"I won't require a bed. I would prefer to stay here."

He wouldn't argue with her over that, not when he'd finally convinced her to stay in safety inside. "Can I bring you some clothing, at least?" He hesitated before asking, "Where are your clothes, if I may ask?"

She lifted her chin, defiance across her face. "Do you truly think I could swim as I do while wearing your ridiculous women's fashions?"

Lucien couldn't help himself. He laughed at that comeback for what felt like the first time since before Emmaline died. It almost hurt to do so, but whether the pain stemmed from his injured body or his laughing muscles being out of shape, he couldn't tell.

When he looked at her, he detected a hint of amusement on her face. Her lips were turned up in a slight smile, and he suspected she was amused by him rather than with him.

"I suppose not," he said. "But I'm trying to be a good host. Can I at least draw a bath for you? This house has running hot water."

Something that looked like desire flashed in her eyes at the mention of hot water, and he knew he'd just zeroed in on something she wanted very much.

"Yes," she said. "I would like that."

"I'll find you something to wear other than the table-cloth," he offered. "Although I should warn you, I only have men's clothes here. Will trousers be sufficient?"

She hesitated again before answering. "Yes. And I'll have you know I only draped it around myself because I know how delicate men's sensibilities are" She gave him a pointed glance, and he felt every ounce of judgement in it. "I was trying to be polite."

Something told him she didn't usually wear clothes at all, and he wasn't sure how he felt about that. He ignored the impulse to dwell on it.

Speaking of politeness… he offered his arm to lead her through the house to the dedicated bathroom. He was suddenly grateful to the surviving Greaves family to have seen a modern bathing room with running water was installed. The electricity might be spotty, but the running water was a true luxury.

She looked at him like he'd gone mad, and he dropped his arm. "Please follow me," he said.

Their footsteps made squishing sounds on the floor, and he cringed, thinking about how much cleaning he would have to do in the morning. Hammond would be very upset to find muddy prints and sodden tablecloths otherwise.

Lucien had dozens of questions for her, but he was only going to press her one issue before the night was out. "May I ask your name?"

She tightened the top of the tablecloth wrapped around her. "Calla."

"Calla what?"

"Just Calla."

So, there would be little formalities between them. They would be Lucien and Calla.

He rather liked that. "It's nice to meet you, Calla. And thank you again for saving my life."

CHAPTER 3

This is so dangerous.

Calla's heartbeat wouldn't slow down to a normal speed, and she had to talk herself out of pushing past Lucien Quinn and bolting out of the house. For one thing, she didn't think she was capable of running on her stupid legs. For another, the lure of hot water was too great to simply brush away.

Calla enjoyed her water-bound existence, and her body was used to the changing temperatures of the sea, but sometimes, heat and warmth were welcome changes.

The memory of struggling to swim in ice water in an indoor tank hit her with all the force of a rogue wave. This time, her stumble wasn't entirely due to walking.

It'll be a tub.

She could handle a tub. She'd never been in one, but she knew what they were.

Is hot water worth putting yourself in danger?

It wasn't just the water, she knew. Or her inability to run. There was the man himself, the utterly insane Lucien Quinn.

Calla knew madmen. Hells, she'd just escaped from one. Lucien, while a different kind of a madman than the one who held her against her will, still qualified as insane. He still had the tablecloth wrapped around himself, although his teeth had stopped chattering, and he led her through his house like nothing was out of the ordinary.

Sane people didn't rush out to the sea in a meager boat during a storm to save someone. Even if she'd been human and drowning, he was still crazy to try to save her.

Crazy and sad. People who had reasons to keep themselves alive didn't do the things he did. She didn't want to give him another reason to want to rush back out to the water, and if she ran right now, he would do that.

She was too busy ruminating over her reasons for putting herself in this situation that she bypassed all the house's features with nary a thought about them. She hadn't even taken note of anything she could use as a landmark in case she had to retrace her steps.

And now, she was faced with a staircase.

Well, fuck.

Lucien had noticed her lumbering gait, and he sent an apologetic look her way. The gas lamps lining the corridor picked out the gold flecks in his green eyes, making them sparkle. "This place doesn't have a lift," he said.

Calla didn't know what that was and shrugged noncommittally in response.

"I could carry you," he offered.

An image of the bedraggled man carrying her up the stairs, like some kind of warrior, popped into her mind. The idea wasn't entirely unpleasant, and she was tempted to take him up on his offer. But she was naked, and humans tended to be skittish about that kind of thing, and she didn't want him to get too close to her right now. She'd managed to hide much of the scarring she'd received at the hands of the man she escaped from with her long hair and tablecloth wrapped around her body and didn't want to invite questions from him about them.

Well, more questions. When he'd fully regained his wits, he would spend more time pondering how the hell she managed to stay alive on a seabed floor.

She had already gripped the banister and started hauling herself up the stairs without answering his question. She was scared if she looked at him right now, she would let him pick her up.

"All right," he murmured and quickly walked ahead of her to lead the way. Louder, he said, "It struck me as odd that the *salle de bain* wouldn't be closer to the kitchen, too."

"I don't know what a *salle de bain* is." She was getting the hang of the stairs and stopped hanging on to the banister for dear life. But why did the staircase have to be so blasted long? Why did it curve in circles? What purpose could that possibly serve?

"Oh? I thought you might be French, based on your accent."

He was fishing for information. She almost giggled at her own bad analogy. *Heh. Fishing and I'm half-fish.* "No."

"My mother was. Hence, my first name."

Once they'd finally ascended the interminable number of stairs, Lucien held open a heavy wooden door stained dark. "It's a bit fancier than what I'm used to," he said. "I grew up bathing in the tub in the kitchen after my parents." He considered something for a couple of seconds. "I still haven't really given myself a chance to explore this house. I was so taken with the subterranean ballroom that I didn't want to leave it."

Calla's curiosity was finally piqued. "This isn't your house?"

"No. I'm not mad enough to have constructed such a

thing, although I will enjoy its amenities while I'm here. You'll be able to manage the taps?"

Calla looked at the brass fixtures joined to the large, beaten copper bathtub. "Yes?"

He heard the question in her voice and demonstrated how to adjust them. "Like this."

She nodded. "Thank you." And then she felt abysmally selfish. "Are you sure you don't want to take a bath first?" At his skeptical look, she added, "I'm used to swimming in the cold. You aren't."

"It won't be a problem," he said, flashing her a smile. "You hauled me out before any damage could be done, and I'm warming up already." He adjusted his tablecloth.

"If you're certain," she said.

"I am. Don't worry about me." He fussed about the room's cabinets for another moment, finally leaving towels for her. He promised to find her some clothing, and then he left.

Calla was finally alone.

She checked the door's lock and made sure it was secure. She found a bar of finely milled soap on a wooden ledge surrounding the tub and sniffed it out of curiosity. The earthy scent of sweet herbs met her nose. She liked it.

She filled the tub, then stared at the water, dreading what was ahead of her.

You've come this far. Get in the damn bathtub.

Bracing herself, she carefully climbed into the water and sank down. She bit back a moan of pleasure as her body met the water's warmth and reached for the soap. She may as well scrub her legs and feet while she still had them.

It would be so much easier if she had more control over her shifting. Once upon a time, before she was captured, she had. But her ability to do that was diminished after her time in captivity, after she was experimented upon.

At least it was less painful, shifting back to her half-fish form. She still had to breathe deeply and remind herself that it wouldn't last forever, but it was infinitely more bearable.

Her scales shifted in color from green to gold under the room's yellow electric lights, and she ran the soap over them. It was the first chance she had to clean herself since before she was kidnapped and the first time she'd been able to enjoy doing so in such decadence. She looked around the room appreciatively, taking in the copper and brass details, the stand holding a wind-up clockwork dryer for her hair, more bars of paper-wrapped soap on a shelf. The tub itself was even big enough to hold her considerable tail fins underwater.

With a relaxed sigh, she dunked her head underwater and cleaned her hair. Ordinarily, she wouldn't bother, but her strange host might find it odd if she left the bathing room still smelling like the sea.

Lucien. His name was Lucien Quinn. And he'd introduced himself as if he should have known who he was. While Calla preferred a solitary life in the water, she still occasionally emerged on land to listen to humans, find out what they knew about her kind. She knew who the current queen was; she knew the names of the major shipping companies and what products they moved. She knew what England was and Scotland. But she'd never heard a word about one Mr. Lucien Quinn.

I've never lured a sailor to his death, though. Murdering human men for fun didn't hold any appeal for her. She couldn't sing worth a damn, either. *If a sailor heard me sing, he'd throw himself overboard before I could get my hands and fins on him.* The notion made her smile.

She stayed in the water until it turned cold, and with a sinking heart, remembered that she would have to shift back to human form. Dread slithered down her spine, and she felt like crying.

She hoped she wouldn't cry when she did it. That would attract attention, and Lucien had already demonstrated that he was willing to save her, no matter the circumstances.

She drained the water, and in the empty tub, concentrated.

This used to be so easy.

The pain wasn't as searing as it was shifting on the beach, but it was still far worse than it used to be. As it was, keeping herself from screaming in agony made her sweat, and tears leaked from her eyes.

Her hair slicked out of her face, her body cleaned, she could now assess the damage she'd sustained in *his* laboratory. Scars crossed her skin in angry red lines along her arms and belly, places where her captor cut into her gills. When she touched fingertips to her neck and throat, she felt raised scar tissue there.

She forced herself to her newly formed feet and, on shaky legs, lifted herself out of the tub. With short, halting steps, she made her way to the looking glass hanging on the wall in an obscenely ornate brass frame and wiped away steam.

She finally had the chance to see what she looked like after so long in that laboratory.

Her dark eyes were huge and red-rimmed from pain and exhaustion. She lifted her hair away to inspect the injuries on her neck and throat and couldn't keep a cry of despair from escaping her.

The scars were so much worse than she thought they'd be. Her golden-green gills on her throat and neck had been hacked away until there was almost nothing left, and while she could see them regrowing, it would be a years-long process. She touched her mangled scales and couldn't keep her tears of grief and rage from falling.

A knock at the door startled her mid-sob.

"Calla? I have some clothes for you."

Of course it was Lucien. Who else would it be? She dragged a hand across her eyes and cleared her throat. "Thank you."

"I'm leaving them outside the door." There was a pause, and he asked, "Are you all right?"

For a second, she wanted to throw open the door and tell him everything that happened: how she'd been caught, what she'd endured. What she was.

The man risked his life for a stranger. He might not be terrified of her or send a telegram to the nearest asylum to pick her up. He might be understanding and compassionate.

But she didn't want to drag him into her mess. "Yes," she called. "I'm fine." As an afterthought, she added, "Thank you for asking."

"I've set out some food in the dining room," he said. "You're welcome to it while I take a bath of my own."

Fuck. He'd been waiting to clean off while she was feeling sorry for herself. "Just a moment," she called. She hurried to the door as best she could and opened it.

Lucien stood before her, a bundle of clothes in his hands and a shocked expression on his face. And she realized she'd forgotten to towel off or at least wrap the tablecloth around herself to keep him from being further scandalized. That was the whole point of raiding the kitchen cupboards for it in the first place.

She took the clothes from him. "Thank you. I won't be much longer."

She quickly dressed in the man's trousers and shirt he left her. They were too large, but she expected that. Lucien towered over her by at least half a foot.

She wrapped her wet hair in a towel and opened the door again. "Thank you," she repeated.

He nodded. "You're welcome. I won't be long, either. Do you remember how to get back to the dining room?"

She racked her brain, trying to recall the route they'd taken. "Downstairs?"

"Downstairs, past a parlor full of porcelain dolls, past a sitting room with a piano, at the end of the corridor," he explained patiently. "There's an oil portrait of a stuffy fellow wearing a white wig at its doorway. I've left sandwiches out, although I'm sure it's getting close to breakfast. I haven't checked the clock lately. Help yourself if you're hungry."

She nodded. Emotion welled up in her at his kindness. "Thank you again."

"I'll be there shortly."

He took her place in the bathing room, leaving her alone. At least this time, she wouldn't have to suffer the indignity of being watched as she struggled with the stairs.

Except going down was easier than up. She sat down on the top step and slid down each one in turn until she reached the first floor.

Now, let's find that dining room.

THE FANCY BATHING room with running water actually had a *shower.* Lucien had to turn a brass hand-crank to get its mechanism to start, but he didn't care about that.

Hot water and a timesaving shower. He didn't understand why the current owner didn't want to live at Greaves Estate.

Hot water, a shower, and the subterranean ballroom. He was finding things to love about this space.

But when he thought of the ballroom, he thought of Calla.

Nothing about her made sense.

He hadn't been shocked by her nudity when she opened the bathroom door. What had left him speechless was the scarring on her body: the injuries were precise and deliberate. Calla had been forced to suffer. Someone had been unspeakably cruel to her, and as he cleaned up, rage welled within him on her behalf.

He would take her to the village constable, he decided. As soon as morning broke. The village *had* to have a constable. And then he'd give her money to take a dirigible or train anywhere she wanted.

He finished his shower and toweled off, then dressed in the set of fresh clothing he brought with him from his bedchamber. Exhaustion pulled at him, and he was still sore from his near-drowning, but he still forced himself to leave the bathroom and meet his guest in the dining room.

He found her there, at the head of the table, delicately picking at a cold roast beef sandwich. Her hair was still wrapped in a towel. "Hello," he said softly.

She still jumped. "Hello to you, too."

Damned if he couldn't place her accent. She definitely wasn't from anywhere in Great Britain. If anything, he'd guess she was from somewhere in continental Europe and learned English when she was young. But which country, he couldn't say.

He sat down next to her and helped himself to a sandwich. "I hope this is sufficient."

She nodded. "This is better than anything I've eaten in days."

"You've hardly touched it."

She lifted her chin in defiance. "I was waiting for you."

His hand hovered over the tray he'd put together, unexpectedly touched by her words. No one had waited for him to start a meal since before Emmaline died; he hadn't shared one with another person since the day of her funeral.

That meal had ended with his reluctantly eating a funeral biscuit at Emmaline's aunt's urging. He hadn't eaten any kind of biscuit since.

To Calla, he said, "Thank you."

They ate in surprisingly companionable silence for a few moments, and when he noticed her looking longingly at the rest of the sandwiches on the tray, he said, "Please help yourself. Would you like some tea?"

She reached for another sandwich, considered his offer, and nodded. "Please."

He left her to go to the kitchen and fix a pot. He boiled water on the kitchen stove, a modern steam-powered thing with a pair of cranks jutting from the side. While he prepared a teapot, he thought about how to broach the subject of the constable with her. He had a feeling she was going to argue against it.

When he returned to the dining room with a tea tray balanced in his hands, she wore the expression of a woman who'd finally eaten enough. Her shirtsleeves—*his* shirtsleeves, really—hung too far over her wrists, and she absentmindedly played with the cuffs.

He took his seat and poured tea for both of them. He took a fortifying sip, unsure how she would react when he brought up the constable.

And something else.

"Calla," he began, setting down his cup. "I couldn't help but notice your injuries earlier."

She turned a sharp gaze to him. "What of them?"

"You don't have to tell me about it if you don't want to," he continued. "But I'm worried for you. I can take you into the village, and you can alert the constable before you leave. I can arrange a dirigible ticket for you." He remembered his journey to the estate. "Well, you would have to pay a carriage driver to take you to the Manchester airfield before proceeding. We're quite far away from civilization here."

"Not far enough," Calla said, but he had the feeling she wasn't addressing the thought to him. "And what do you mean, the Manchester airfield?"

Lucien stilled. "That's the nearest place to board a dirigible."

"Oh. Yes, of course. And I can get to Scotland from there?"

"To Edinburgh or Inverness. There's a very small one in Dundee, as well. Those are the only airfields in Scotland."

Calla's lips hovered over the rim of her cup. "I see."

"What's in Scotland, if I may ask?"

"It's far away," she replied. "It's the furthest place I can think of."

"It's still in Great Britain," Lucien said. His concern for her deepened further, which he hadn't known possible.

Her swimming at night during a storm, nude. Her injuries. Her manner of speech, her lack of very basic geographical knowledge all spelled out what a terrible way she was in. Had she sustained a head injury, too?

"Calla," he said, hoping she picked up on the urgency

in his voice. "I can help you. *Please* let me help you. Who did this to you?"

Her answer was far too quick to be sincere. "No one."

"'No one' left you naked in the sea at night, 'no one' left you with those scars? I can plainly see you've been tortured. Whoever did this doesn't deserve to get away with it!"

She slammed down her cup with such force Lucien was surprised it didn't break. "I will take your offer of a dirigible ticket now."

Oh, hell. He'd offered that with no strings attached. "Do you know how to get to Manchester?"

"You've already told me," she snapped. "Hire a carriage to take me to the airfield. I can manage that."

"Calla, how do you spell your name?"

She froze. He thought he could see her panic coming to life in her eyes, and he immediately regretted asking.

He was a writer. He didn't often come across the illiterate in his ever-shrinking social and professional circles. But even the few illiterate people he'd met in his life could spell their names.

She looked like she wanted to slap him.

But she didn't. Instead, she said, "I would like to leave now."

"Of course." Lucien had grossly overstepped his bounds. He would regret asking her how to spell her name for the rest of his life. "Let me fix you some food first, to take with you."

"Why are you still helping me?"

The question was unexpected, her voice harsh, and shame washed over him at the unkind question he'd just asked her. "As I've already told you, you saved my life," he said. "And I insulted you. Putting together a basket of sandwiches and biscuits is the least I can do. I'm sorry."

Before she could interrogate him further, he stood up, his interest in the tea gone. He picked up the sandwich tray and brought it back to the kitchen, then set about looking for a suitable basket to wrap up the leftovers for her journey. He didn't know how to get to the village, but Hammond had said it was nearby, and there was bound to be a map in the study.

But a pale blur shot past him, interrupting his thoughts, and aimed straight for the servants' door.

"Calla," he said. A mixture of alarm and exasperation threaded through him as she threw open the door. He didn't have to look in the dining room to see her borrowed clothes and hair towel in a crumpled heap on the floor.

He ran after her. Her steps were clumsier than his, but she had a head start, and he could see her sheer determination in escaping.

And truthfully, he couldn't bring himself to force what he thought was best on her.

So, he stopped and watched as she stumbled a little over the grass and pebble beach and gracefully dove into the dark water.

How COULD she have forgotten that she couldn't read?

The cold water muffled Calla's choked sob as she swam as quickly as she could, her lower body recognizing the water and shifting almost immediately. She welcomed the pain the shift brought, a temporary distraction from her anger at her own stupidity.

Lucien had asked her to spell her own name, and she couldn't. She wouldn't be able to navigate a trip to Scotland on a dirigible or know how to find a carriage to take her to the airfield. She didn't know Scotland had so many of them or the names of its cities. She knew less than nothing about how to live and move around on land.

Just like she knew almost nothing about moving through the sea anymore. She'd been sure that as the water grew colder, she was swimming further north, but that proved to be untrue.

She screamed in frustration, sending ripples into the water.

Calla had been exiled from her fellow mermaids. She had no home, no friends or family. She'd run away from the only person who had shown her any kindness. She had nothing.

She let herself float to the water's surface. The sun had started to rise, and she let herself enjoy the sight for a few moments.

And then she spotted something floating a few feet away. She recognized it as the boat Lucien capsized from.

She dragged her arm over her eyes, a useless gesture to wipe away her tears, as she watched the little boat bob in the water.

The least she could do was return it to him. She would leave it on the shore for him to find. It was the polite thing to do after he'd let her use his bathtub and fed her.

She swam to the boat and gripped its wooden side, and turned back in the direction of Lucien's house.

Calla wasn't sure how long she swam until the weird spires of his house came into view, but the sun steadily rose as she did. The water nearly glowed under its light, warming it a little. There was no way for her to haul the boat while swimming underwater, so she held her head above it, dragging the boat behind her as she swam closer to shore.

A familiar figure waited on the beach.

Her breath caught, and for a few seconds, she considered leaving the boat in his view and diving back underwater. Wouldn't that be the easiest thing to do? He would be one less human who knew about the existence of mermaids.

But Calla was so tired of being alone. She was tired of running away. She had received an offer of help she could ill afford to refuse.

She took a deep breath of air and felt the shredded remains of the gills on her neck constrict in response. It was as if her own body was confirming that her idea to ask him for help was a good one.

It was the *only* idea she had.

He didn't move toward her as she swam closer, undoubtedly wary of ever getting in the water again. "Hello," she called out. When the water became too shallow for her to swim comfortably in, she pushed the boat forward, taking care to keep her lower body underwater. The boat floated uselessly a few feet from the shore. "I found this."

Lucien regarded her silently, a fresh cup of tea in his hands. He looked like he couldn't believe she'd reappeared.

"I owe you an apology," she began. "You helped me when you didn't have to, and I was afraid and ran away. I can't read."

His expression softened. "That's unfortunately common."

"It's not just that." Tears threatened her again, and she willed them away. Crying would get her nowhere. "Everything you said about my injuries—you're correct, I was tortured. But you wouldn't believe me if I told you why.

"And then I saw your boat, and I thought you'd want it back," she continued. "And you've been kind to me, and humans aren't usually kind."

"Humans?" A shadow crossed Lucien's face.

"Yes." She forced herself further along the pebbled seabed until he could see her tail and fins through the water.

Shock suffused his features. He dropped his teacup.

"I'm a mermaid."

CHAPTER 4

"*I*'m a mermaid."

Calla spoke the words with a shyness he hadn't heard from her yet. The green-gold scales of her tail shimmered under the rising sun on the water like jewels, each of her fins at the bottom of her tail the size of his hands. The scars on her upper body stood out in stark relief against the otherworldly beauty of her scales, reminding Lucien of the horrors she must have endured.

Not knowing what else to do, Lucien plunked down on the pebbled beach, as close as he could get to her without actually stepping into the water. He thought if he had to continue standing, his knees might give way beneath him.

He said the first thing that came to mind: "Are you sure?"

Calla laughed, the first time he'd heard her do such a thing. It was the first time he'd seen her smile, and it transformed her face. For a few seconds, she looked like the mythical creature she was.

But just as quickly, her laughter evaporated. "Yes," she said. "I'm very sure. Doesn't my being one make sense?"

He parroted her answer. "Yes."

She hauled herself through the shallow water until she sat next to him, tail straight out ahead of her. The water lapped at her fins. "You'll get your trousers wet again," Calla said.

Lucien hardly cared about a little water dampening his trousers. "They can be laundered. I would've had to go back in to fetch the boat if it floated back this way, anyway. I'm sure the caretaker would have a fit if it went missing."

He couldn't believe he was having this conversation, that he was sitting half in the water with a real mermaid. Part of him thought he might have actually drowned the night before.

"Can you pinch me?" he asked.

Calla tilted her head to the side quizzically. "Why?"

"I'm not quite sure I didn't die last night."

She gave a small shrug of her shoulders and obliged. "Damn it," Lucien muttered, rubbing the pinched spot on his arm. "Thank you, I suppose."

"You didn't die last night," she said.

"I know, and I'm not dreaming, either." He stared at the water. The boat bobbed in it a little, and Calla reached for it to keep it from floating away. "Why did you come back?"

"Because I can't read."

She turned huge, beseeching eyes to him, and with the look, something twisted in his gut. She was in trouble; that much was obvious.

Calla continued, words tumbling from her in a rush. "What you said to me about the dirigible and the places they go… I had no idea. I just heard about Scotland and how far away it was, and I thought it might be the other side of the world. And that was where I needed to go."

"Who are you running from?" Lucien asked, keeping his voice as gentle as he could.

"I was exiled by my people and had to leave their waters," she said, voice halting. "I've been alone for a while, and I was taken not too long ago by someone obsessed with…" She faltered before continuing. "Creatures like me. He experimented on me. He cut off my gills. I can still breathe without them, but you see what he did."

She lifted away her wet hair just enough to show him a row of meticulously placed straight lines along the side of her neck, just under her ear. Tiny green gills had started to regrow at irregular intervals, but even Lucien could tell they would likely never fully heal. She would bear those scars for the rest of her life.

"Who was this man?" Lucien asked.

"Are you going to notify the constable?" There was a mocking note to her tone, but he suspected it was a defense mechanism for her.

"I don't know," he replied honestly. "You've been hurt. You could make a report without telling him you're a mermaid."

"I don't even know where he is or where he kept me," Calla said. "I know his name but nothing else."

"What is it?"

"Isadore."

"Do you know his surname?"

Calla gave him a look that clearly questioned his intelligence. "No. He kept me in a tank in a laboratory in a warehouse near a dock. I escaped by chance when he left it unlocked one night. I shifted into my human form and jumped in the harbor."

Lucien's mind worked quickly, trying to figure out how to parse identifying information from her about her assailant.

"He sounded different from you," Calla continued. "But still the same. Does that make sense? I've noticed that quite a bit from English sailors." She paused. "I've never killed one if you're wondering."

"Hadn't crossed my mind. I was thinking about how to locate the man who did this to you."

"You could help me?" Her face lit up with hope.

"Of course. I already offered to earlier." Who cared a whit about a stupid adventure novel when he'd long ago lost the passion for writing? Helping Calla was a worthier endeavor than staring at blank sheets of paper for hours. "You'll tell me about this Isadore, and I'll figure out where he could be based on your descriptions. I'll teach you to read enough to take a dirigible journey as well if you like."

"You know how to read?"

"I write books." He caught himself in the half-truth. "Well, I used to. I'm renting this place because I have to finish one, and I'm in danger of missing my deadline." It wouldn't be the first time, so he added, "Again."

"That's why you expected I should know your name when you introduced yourself."

"I'm not quite a household name, but my books are popular enough, I suppose. I earn a living from them."

But Lucien didn't want to talk about his impending deadline or his writing at all. He needed to know more about Calla's predicament, how to save her.

"Would you prefer to stay in the sea?" he asked. "You're welcome to share Greaves Estate with me, but I don't know how to accommodate a mermaid's needs. I can bring you meals if you'd rather stay in the water."

She could see hesitation warring on her face, plain as day.

"You don't have to decide straight away," he said. "I'm spending my time in the subterranean ballroom while I try to finish this bloody epistle before my editor has enough and has me murdered. Merely tap on the glass if you need anything."

"I'll stay with you," she said. "I can shift into human form. It would be good to exercise my legs. I'm not so good at walking, as I'm sure you've noticed."

"You can run just fine. You demonstrated that this morning."

"It was dark, and I surprised you," she said. "I was frightened. And I don't think you ran as quickly as you could."

"I was recovering from nearly drowning. I still am. And I didn't want to frighten you further." He could hardly believe everything that had happened over the course of just a few hours. "Shall I give you some privacy to, uh, shift? I'll bring you some clothing."

She nodded. "Thank you."

Lucien rose to his feet and, spotting his dropped teacup, picked it up. He crossed the grass separating the beach from the back of the house and let himself in.

The clothes she had shed on her mad run from him were still in the dining room. He'd mechanically folded them after she ran off, a tangible reminder of his bizarre brush with death, and had stared at them a couple of times since in shock. He gathered them and brought them back to her.

She had shifted her lower body and was struggling to rise to her feet on unsteady legs. Lucien reached out his free hand, and she grabbed it with surprising strength.

He held out the clothes, averting his eyes as she slipped on the shirt and trousers. His offering her clothing wasn't for the benefit of keeping the neighbors from being scandalized; there wasn't a neighbor for miles. Nor was it for him. He just wanted her to know he saw her as a person.

"Does it hurt?" he asked.

"It's excruciating." She leaned on him as they made a slow walk back to the house.

"For someone who claims illiteracy, your vocabulary is amazing."

She gave a half-shrug at his statement. "My people can speak the language. I listen to humans when I'm near them. Isadore also spoke to me often. I can recognize some letters, but I just can't put them in any proper order. And it depends on how the letter's written. Does that make sense?"

"Perfectly. It'll be easier to teach you to read than I thought."

She changed the subject. "Scotland's far away, isn't it?"

"Not as far as, say, the Americas, but far enough. Why is that the place you want to escape to?"

"It's the furthest place I know on land," she said. "But now you've told me how much bigger the world is, and I don't know where to go now."

"Can't you return to your mermaid family?" he asked. "You mentioned you were exiled. Could you…"

She cut him off. "No. I can't return to them. Exile is forever."

"I'm familiar with the definition, but if they're your family," he began, but she interrupted him again.

"No."

He wouldn't argue with her. Instead, he felt like a fool. Of course, mermaid society would be very different from human society.

Not so different, a little voice reminded him. *Think of Emmaline. Think of what she gave up.*

It wasn't quite the same as what Calla endured, but Emmaline certainly bore the brunt of her decision to marry Lucien instead of that dour viscount, twenty years her senior, that her parents picked for her.

Lucien held open the servants' door for her, and she hobbled over the threshold. "Are you hungry?" he asked.

"Why do I get the feeling that you try to fix everything with food?"

"I thought you might want something to eat, is all. What do mermaids usually eat?"

"Fish, sea plants. Probably ones you've never seen."

"Is there anything you hate?" he asked. "A cook comes by twice a week. I'm sure I can ask her to make things you like." He paused. "I haven't met her yet, but that seems to be in a cook's wheelhouse."

He set about making a new cup of tea to replace the one he dropped. When she didn't reply, he turned to face her. Her expression was wary. "Calla? Is there anything else you want me to know that you haven't told me about?"

"Why are you being so kind to me?"

She had asked that before her mad dash back to the sea, and the question was painful to hear again. His reasons for doing so sprang to his mind.

Because he couldn't leave someone out to fend for herself when she'd been tortured and experimented upon.

Because the man who did that to her was still out there, possibly preying on other mermaids who just wanted to be left alone.

Because she was illiterate.

Because he knew the chances of turning in his book on time were slim, and he would rather the time not spent writing go toward helping someone else instead of feeling sorry for himself.

Because he recognized another lost, lonely soul.

"You need help," he said. "I'm able to provide it."

"At what cost to me?"

That was a fair and astute question for her to ask. "None. I have the means, and I can share them. Like you, I have no one else."

Her face visibly relaxed at his words.

"I can make you some breakfast," he continued. "Take a seat in the dining room, and I'll be there shortly."

RELIEF AND TREPIDATION poured through Calla as she sat, ramrod straight, in the same fussy chair she'd taken earlier in the morning. Or the middle of the night; she'd lost track of time.

Her whole body hurt after shifting so many times in a matter of hours. For the first time in her life, she wasn't sure if she could shift back to her mermaid form when she wanted to, at least not for a while, and the feeling of not being in control of her own body was terrifying.

She took in her surroundings: the dark wooden furniture, a cabinet holding an array of clockwork children's toys, the paintings of sour-faced old men wearing white wigs lining the walls. The carpet beneath the table and her feet was irregularly striped black and white in a pattern that made her dizzy if she looked at it too long. So, she turned away from it.

What was she going to do next?

Lucien had offered to help her, and strangely, she believed he would. He'd already tried when he nearly drowned himself. There were things about himself that he wasn't telling her, the reasons for his odd, misplaced altruism, and Calla found herself determined to learn why.

Why did he have a death wish? No one who wanted to live would rush out to open water, in the middle of the night, during a storm, to save a stranger that any reasonable person would have left alone. Sane people didn't see someone on the seabed floor and try to save them.

He woke me up. If he hadn't flashed that fucking light in my eyes, I would've stayed asleep.

But it wasn't just his light that alerted him to her presence. She'd been lured to his subterranean ballroom by its lights like a common fish, shedding all sense of caution as she did so. They'd looked friendly and welcoming in her exhausted state.

"I hope you like poached eggs."

Calla looked up from staring at the tabletop, lost in thought. "I don't know."

Lucien set a plate before her holding a white blob on a slice of toasted bread and another containing the same at the place next to her. "My mother made sure I could cook for myself and read a recipe before I..." He faltered. "Before I got married. I'm not a French chef, but I'm good enough, I suppose. My wife appreciated it."

Sadness tinged his words when he spoke about marriage. "Where is your wife now?" Calla asked. "Wouldn't she have liked to join you here?"

"She passed away," Lucien replied curtly. "Just over two years ago." His fingers tightened around his fork.

"I'm sorry."

"Thank you." He dug into his toast and egg, and Calla did likewise, not wanting to be any more rude than she already had been. After he'd swallowed a bite, he said, "It's strange, telling someone 'thank you' after expressing condolences, isn't it?"

Before she could respond, he continued. "That's all we're really allowed to say when someone close to you has died, or you're speaking to another who is grieving. 'I'm sorry' and 'thank you.' We don't like to talk about the person herself for fear it reopens healing wounds. We wear mourning instead of talking about the deceased."

Calla didn't know how to reply. "I don't know what mourning is."

"It's a ridiculous practice of wearing black clothing for a specific period of time after someone close to you passes. I wore black for eighteen months. I still feel like wearing it."

"Is the grief supposed to disappear after you stop wearing all black?"

"A perfectly logical question," he said. "Yes, it is. But no, it doesn't."

"You must have loved your wife very much," Calla said.

"I did." He looked around the room, then at Calla. "I miss her every day. She would have loved this place. There's a study that the caretaker hinted that I'm supposed to use, but it reminds me too much of Emmaline, dead insects and all. She had a morbid streak to her that I didn't share. So, I'm trying to write in the subterranean ballroom."

Dead insects? Morbid streak? What in the hells did he mean by that? Calla sidestepped that tidbit of information. "Have you written anything?"

"Ah, there it is. Changing the subject. It fits right in with wearing mourning."

Oh, she was bad at this. "I wanted to know about your writing. Is your difficulty with it seems connected to your wife's passing?"

"It is," he said. He ate the last of his toast, and Calla remembered the food in front of her and ate another bite. She decided that while edible, a poached egg wasn't the best thing she'd ever eaten. "And I apologize. I know all of this is new to you, and it is for me, too. I don't speak of Emmaline that often anymore."

"Because you're expected to have moved on," Calla offered.

His green eyes regarded her thoughtfully for a few seconds, and she felt herself unexpectedly blush. "Are all mermaids this astute and blunt?"

She smiled. "No."

"Is that why you were exiled?"

"Is this your way of getting me to talk about a difficult time in my life?"

"No, it was a poor attempt at conversation." Now it was his turn to change the subject. "What kind of accommodations do you require? How often do you have to shift yourself?"

Calla thought for a few seconds, trying to remember the last time she'd spent extended time in human form. The last time had to have been a couple of years ago, when she spent a couple of nights with a human sailor on shore leave, to satisfy a strange carnal curiosity about humans. That had proved to be disastrous and the reason she was in the position she was presently in. "I don't know. I could stay this way indefinitely if I wanted to. I think."

"I'm afraid that for all the strange features of this house, it doesn't have a pool. Will a regular bedroom be sufficient?"

"I've never slept on a human bed, but I'm willing to try." She hadn't slept during those nights with the sailor on that bed; that wasn't the point. "I can take breaks in the sea, anyway. Stretch my fins, so to speak. I'll wave to you while you're writing in the ballroom."

She appreciated his trying to make her comfortable. Somehow, she suspected that he would be easy to distract while he tried to write. The thought of tapping at the ballroom glass to get his attention—a reversal of the glass aquarium experience—made her smile a little.

But the thought of a glass aquarium reminded her of Isadore's tank, and she felt it fade.

"What is it?" Lucien asked.

She shook her head. "Nothing."

He didn't press her, which she also appreciated.

His breakfast complete, he stood up to clear his plate. Calla quickly finished her poached egg and toast and did likewise. He reached for her dishes, but she shook her head. "I can help," she said. "I'm not completely ignorant of human ways."

She followed him back to the kitchen. "How much time have you spent with us on land?" he asked.

"More than I should have," Calla replied.

"I'm compelled to remind you that your English is excellent."

"I told you my people speak it," she explained. "Not as well as the English do. We live near English waters and occasionally follow English ships, after all." She thought for a moment, then added, "We do have our own language, but we hear English so often that we speak it, too."

"You also mentioned you haven't killed any sailors with your seductive songs, but you speak to them?" Lucien took her dishes and put them in the sink to wash them. Calla watched as he twisted the copper taps, and when she tried to help, he shooed her away.

Calla felt herself flush when he said "seductive." It was innocent enough coming from him, but it still put an image in her mind that he wouldn't share with her. "Just the act of my singing could kill a man. I'm terrible at it."

He laughed.

Calla stared at him, fascinated. He smiled easily. She thought he must've done that a lot before his wife died.

Once upon a time, I used to smile and laugh a lot, too.

Before her exile and her condemnation of aimlessly swimming around England's harbors, stealing glances at sailors and the other people who crowded the docks. Until that day she got herself captured.

She forced that thought from her mind and focused on Lucien, who now smiled at her with a twinkle in his eye he hadn't had before. He dried the dishes and put them away in a cupboard that held a shockingly few number of plates for the size it was. But Lucien had already explained the house was rented, meant to be temporary.

"Are you tired at all?" he asked.

Calla was always tired these days, but she didn't want to heap her troubles on him any more than she already had. "Yes. I'm sure you are, too. You had a difficult night."

"I'll be fine," he said. "You have a lot more to heal from."

Calla had to resist the impulse to cover the scars with her hair. He didn't care if she had them, and he was right.

She hadn't relaxed in years, always trying to stay out of her people's waters, always trying to stay as unnoticed as possible by humans when she was in her mermaid form. And she had done a spectacular job of fucking that up.

"Will you be all right taking the stairs to your room?" Lucien asked.

"Is there another way I could get up them?"

"I could carry you."

She waited for him to laugh again, but he looked perfectly serious. She had felt the muscles under his clothes when she dragged him out of the sea and knew he possessed considerable strength under his sensible gray trousers and white shirt. He would be able to carry her up the stairs, and she would probably like it. When was the last time anyone had taken care of her?

She wanted to say yes, but she knew he was still in rough shape after his capsizing. Besides, she had to learn how to walk steadily on her own, and that included managing a spiral staircase.

"No, thank you," she said. "I'll manage."

She thought she saw disappointment flash in his eyes for a few seconds, but it quickly disappeared. "Follow me."

CHAPTER 5

*L*ucien flipped through his pages of foolscap before stacking them back together in a neat pile. He picked it up and hefted their weight, convinced the sheets felt heavier when they were covered in his tidy handwriting. He was a lot of things, but a possessor of poor penmanship wasn't one of them.

He'd written forty-one pages since Calla went to sleep over a day ago.

Lucien checked on her a few times during the previous day and night, secure in the big, fluffy bed in the room down the corridor from his. She'd crawled into bed, still clad in his too-large clothes, and had slept ever since.

He was unsure what to do about that: medical training was far beyond his realm of expertise, let alone the kind of treatment a supernatural being might require.

Guiltily, he wondered if his productive streak had come about because she was in the house with him. He didn't want to think that a suffering person's presence had a positive effect on his creativity.

Or, perhaps his original idea of a change of scenery worked.

He tucked the pages into a leather folder embossed with his initials, a gift from Emmaline when they married, and set it on the chair next to him. He adjusted the music stand he'd been using as a makeshift desk into its proper position and stood up to stretch his legs. He began to pace the length of the subterranean ballroom to clear his head.

He couldn't believe he got so much work done. The possibility of finishing his book and sending it to his editor on time tantalizingly danced before him.

"Why does every staircase in this house have to be circular? How are you not dizzy all the time?"

He smiled and turned around to see Calla, gripping the gaudy, looping brass railing as she descended the ballroom's staircase. Her gait was improved from the day before, but she still moved slowly as she turned around and around on the stairs. "Did you sleep well?"

"Better than I have in years, thank you."

"You slept for over a day. You must have needed the rest."

She lifted her gaze from where she'd been keeping them on her feet. She paused on the stair she was on, eyes wide. "I slept for a day and night?"

"Over twenty-four hours, all told, but there isn't a clock down here for me to tell you exactly how long. I checked in on you a few times to make sure you were all right."

"Why did you let me sleep that long?" She resumed her careful trip down the stairs.

"I thought it would be rude to wake you up. I'm also unfamiliar with mermaids' sleeping habits."

She shuffled off the last step and made a few tentative, halting steps toward him. He moved closer in time to catch her when she tripped over the too-long legs of her borrowed trousers. "Fuck!" she said into his chest.

Lucien couldn't help himself at the epithet and said, "Good God!" before helping her to her feet.

She looked chastised for all of a second before she smiled and said, "When I speak to humans, I speak to sailors. I'm surprised I haven't said it before now."

"I'm not upset, just surprised. It isn't a word I hear often."

"I suppose you wouldn't." She looked past Lucien's shoulder at the ballroom's glass walls. She hobbled closer to the nearest one, although Lucien noticed her gait had improved since yesterday. She touched the glass in wonder as she stared at the gently waving water outside. The tide was out, and a few inches of crisp blue sky visible. "This room is amazing. I've never seen anything like it."

"Neither have I. When I wanted to get away from London, I wanted something the polar opposite of what I have there."

"What's your home in London like?"

"It's a flat," he explained. "It isn't extravagant, but there's more than enough space for me. It lacks both a subterranean ballroom and a bowling room, although I must admit I haven't made any use of the bowling room."

"I don't know what a bowling room is."

"It's a game," he explained. "The objective is to knock things over with a ball. I'll show you later."

Calla nodded her head toward the orchestra pit and its chairs pulled out of place. "What's that?"

"My new writing space. Officially, it's an orchestra pit." At Calla's blank expression, he added, "This room was meant for parties. That's where the musicians would play."

"Oh."

"And I've been writing there." Pride surged through

him, and he crossed the distance to the orchestra pit to retrieve his work. "I actually got some work done." He opened his writing folder and pulled out the manuscript. "Over forty pages." He held them out to her.

Too late, he'd forgotten she couldn't read.

But Calla accepted them anyway and cautiously held them, flipping through the sheets of paper. "You wrote this?"

He nodded.

She ran her fingers over his words. "I've never seen this before. It's beautiful."

"My handwriting? I can take pride in my penmanship in addition to writing adventure stories."

"What kind of adventure stories?"

"Flights of fancy for young people, mostly. Stories about traveling to the stars or the bottom of the ocean, or traveling through time."

"I wish I could read something like that." She held the pages closer to her face, studying the loops and swirls of his handwriting. "How did you do this?"

Lucien gestured to the orchestra pit. "Sit down, and I'll show you."

They settled on chairs next to each other, and he adjusted the positions of the music stands in front of them. He removed a sheet of paper from the stack he kept under the chair he'd designated as his and set it in front of her with a pencil.

She looked at the paper and then at him, expectation on her face.

Perhaps she had never seen writing in action. Leaning over, he picked up the sheet, the smell of her hair reaching his nose and giving him pause.

He expected a mermaid would smell of the sea, and the scent of water clung to her. But beneath it was something else he couldn't identify, something unique that was all Calla, and it was a distraction he hadn't anticipated.

He shook his head a little as if to remind himself that noticing how her hair smelled was inappropriate, and he turned back to the paper. He wrote his name, and below it, hers. He gave the pencil and sheet back to her. "The top says 'Lucien Quinn,'" he said. "Below, it says 'Calla.' Here, you try it out."

Calla stared at the names, a smile on her face. Taking the pencil in her right hand, she tried to mimic his handwriting and failed. But that didn't faze her: she dragged the pencil in a pattern across the page, doodling until she'd sketched an irregular curlicue. "Can I keep this?" she asked, holding up the paper.

"Of course. You can have more paper if you like. I'm sure there are plenty of spare pencils and pens somewhere in this place." Except there was one thing he meant to do first. Taking the page from her again, he printed their names in block letters below the handwritten ones. "You may find this easier to start off with reading," he explained.

"That looks like the letters I've seen before."

"And that's what a dirigible ticket would be printed with." He fetched another sheet of paper and wrote the alphabet in block letters. He was making things up as he went along; he'd never taught anyone to read before, and he wasn't sure how to go about it. "This is the alphabet. Several languages use it, including English, of course. All of our written words are made up of these letters, twenty-six of them."

Calla looked at her name, printed on her doodled sheet of paper, and back to the alphabet, carefully checking the spelling of her name and his. Holding her pencil in her fist as a child might, she carefully copied the letters spelling out his name. She slid the paper to his music stand, a triumphant smile on her face. "There."

"But do you know what it says? I still haven't explained what each letter is and how it sounds."

"I know it says 'Lucien Quinn.' You told me what it says, and I thought you'd like that the first thing I wrote myself is your name." She arched a dark eyebrow at him, challenging him to contradict her.

Unexpected emotions warred through him at her revelation, a combination of alarm and flattery. "Now write yours," he said quickly. "Your own name is important."

Calla gave him a look that said she didn't understand his reasoning but dutifully wrote her name below his, the letters uneven and uncertain.

It was a start.

～

CALLA ADMIRED her handiwork before re-folding the paper he'd given her and slipping it back into the pocket of her borrowed trousers.

Lucien had returned to his writing, and not wanting to disturb him, she left him to his own devices in the subterranean ballroom and decided to explore the rest of the house. And as much as her fingers itched to touch everything, she kept her hands in her pockets to resist temptation.

The house was massive, far too large for just one or two people, but there was always something new for her to look at. She took note of her steps in case she had to backtrack as she padded barefoot through the myriad rooms and corridors.

She felt unexpectedly and blessedly safe in this space,

something she'd never thought to experience again since her exile.

Calla limped along a corridor, peeking into rooms whose doors were open and gawking at the sheer amount of tchotchkes and artwork arranged in each one. She recognized more objects than she expected; like all mermaids, she'd witnessed an occasional shipwreck, and she did come across sunken boats on seabeds during her travels. One had been her temporary home for a time after she was exiled.

She did make an exception to her no-touching rule when she reached the room full of books and a desk.

She ran her finger along the books' spines, imagining the words inside them, the stories they contained. *Had Lucien written any of them?* She removed the folded paper from her pocket and compared his carefully written name with the words embossed on the spines but didn't see anything that matched.

She let herself admire the books for another few moments before looking around the rest of the room. Collections of dead insects, pierced through with pins and enclosed in glass-fronted boxes, lined the walls, and the sight of them sent a shudder rippling through her. Who would do such a thing? The butterflies were pretty, and those that weren't were just trying to live and spin webs in peace.

They reminded her of herself, trapped in a tank.

She quickly left the room, nearly tripping over her own clumsy feet in her haste, until she reached the stairs.

Calla looked up through its spiral shape, hating it, and decided there was nothing worth exploring up there right now, anyway. She forged on, selecting a corridor she hadn't been down before.

The door at its end was open, and she poked her head inside. "What the hell?" she muttered.

The floor was pale bare wood, its polish shinier than anything she'd seen in the house so far, gleaming in the sunlight that streamed through the high windows. Part of the floor was sectioned off with raised edges, forming a perfectly straight lane in the center of the room. At the very end was a collection of bottles arranged in a triangular pattern. When Calla investigated, she found the "bottles" to be made of wood.

"You found the bowling lane."

Lucien's voice startled her, and she dropped the one she'd been holding. "What the hell is this?" she asked, righting the bottle.

"It's for bowling. It's a game." Lucien opened a cabinet on his end of the room, looking for something. He hefted a large ball in his hands. "The object is to push down all the pins with a ball."

He clearly wanted to demonstrate how the game worked, and Calla stepped out of the way, joining him at his end. Lucien lowered the ball in his hands before sending it on a crooked path to the end, where it knocked over a few of the things he'd called pins.

"What's the point of knocking down the pins?" she asked.

He shrugged, the sunlight picking up the gold in his sandy hair as he did so. "For fun."

"Are you supposed to knock down all of them or just a few?"

He was already walking down the lane, presumably to right the pins. He tossed a mischievous smile over his shoulder as he did so, and Calla thought he might have just given her a glimpse into the playful man he used to be. "You didn't know what this game was until five minutes ago, so I know you aren't being facetious," he replied. He moved to right the pins, but as he reached down, he spotted something. "Ah."

"What is it?"

Lucien pulled a lever Calla hadn't noticed until he touched it and stepped back. A hydraulic, steamy hiss sounded, and a brass arm extended from the wall behind the lane. It automatically reset the pins, then recessed back into the wall.

"A steam-powered pin... setter, I suppose it's called," said Lucien. He sounded a little in awe of it. "I'm surprised the current owners of the house thought to have this installed. Or perhaps another relative or the caretaker did it when they turned this place into a rental property." He hurried back to where Calla stood, the ball in his hands. "I can take a look later for a proper rule book, but the gist of the game is to knock down as many pins as you can, with the fewest number of times rolling the ball. Whoever does so wins the game. It's your turn to try." He handed the ball to Calla.

Her hands sank with the unexpected weight of it, and she nearly dropped it on her bare feet. "Fuck!" she exclaimed before she could stop herself.

But Lucien didn't appear scandalized to hear her say curse. "Like this," he said. He moved behind her just enough to adjust her hands' position around the ball. He urged her a little further down the lane in tiny, shuffling steps. "Hold it in one hand as best you can," he said. "Pull your arm back, put some strength into it, and let the ball go."

Calla did as he instructed, very conscious of the feel of his breath against her hair, and released the ball. It moved down the lane slower than it had for Lucien, and it knocked over a paltry two pins before coming to a full stop. "Pathetic," she said.

Lucien reset the pins and retrieved the ball before sending it soaring down the lane again. This time, he managed to knock over three pins before it rolled to the lane's side. "Have you played this before?" Calla asked.

"Twice, and I was half-drunk while I did it. I was acquainted with someone who enjoyed lawn bowls. I've never played inside. I'm not terribly familiar with the rules, as I was drinking the last time I heard them, but the object *is* to knock down the pins."

That put them on relatively equal footing as far as bowling went.

Lucien gave her the ball again, and this time she was better prepared to accept its weight. She lined up the ball with the centermost pin and, putting all of her strength into it, let it fly down the lane.

Every pin crashed to the floor. "I did it!" she exclaimed, surprised.

It was a little thing, but for the first time in a very long time, Calla was proud of herself.

CHAPTER 6

a few companionable days passed, with Lucien writing the days away and Calla occasionally doodling and drawing in the chair next to him in the subterranean ballroom. Sometimes she bowled by herself, and she declared it the most fun she'd ever had on dry land, and she took a couple of breaks to shift and swim in the sea for a few hours. She would tap on the ballroom's glass walls to wave and smile, and every time she did it, Lucien's breath caught.

It wasn't that she was naked and had a tail and fins when she did it that caught his fascination. It was everything else: her effortless movement in the water that reminded him of the grace of the ballet dancers he saw perform *The Swans* at the Alhambra Theatre years ago when he and Emmaline were newly married. It was the way her hair floated around her, just as peaceful as she was as she swam alongside the glass walls.

Her walking skills had dramatically improved as well and continued strengthening even after she spent time shifted in her mermaid form. When she showed Lucien her drawings, he could see she was quickly developing enough skill and strength to start learning to write. And she appeared to be left-handed, he noted. She'd tried holding a pencil in each of her hands at different times, and she definitely favored the left. She did with the bowling ball and eating utensils as well.

Watching Calla now, as the sun rose higher in the noontime sky, or as high as it could get in this part of northern England, he realized something he should have earlier.

She had no clothes.

She'd been borrowing his since she decided to stay with him, and it struck him when he dressed that day that he was down to his last set of clean clothing. Greaves Estate had a very modern automatic clothes washer, but the wardrobe he brought for his tenancy was limited, and she needed her own things. He felt guilty at using so much water for the washer so often, anyway.

Lucien would have to venture into the village and see if there was an establishment that sold women's clothes. He'd been meaning to for a while, the idea in the back of his mind, but he hadn't acted on the impulse since he had actually settled into the estate to write.

He set aside his book and stood up, stretching, and shook out the cramp that formed in his hand. Calla was still swimming near the ballroom, and he tapped the glass wall nearest her to gain his attention.

Her head whirled around, and she met his gaze immediately. He knew she probably couldn't hear him with her ears, but she explained that she picked up vibrations, much like a fish did. She smiled and swam to him, and Lucien said the words, "Meet me at the beach." He enunciated as clearly as he could.

It worked. She nodded and swam upward, and Lucien left the ballroom and headed outside.

She had already hauled herself to the pebbles when he arrived, still sitting in the water in her mermaid form with her elbows balanced on the place where her knees were when she was in her fully human form. The sun picked up the golden highlights in her wet hair, and for a few seconds, the sight reminded Lucien of the mermaid in Hans Christian Andersen's fairy tale.

"I'm heading to the village," Lucien said by way of greeting. "I want to buy you some things."

Calla nodded, understanding immediately. "You want your clothing back." She inclined her head to the grass, where his folded-up shirt and trousers waited for her.

"Yes. I mean, no, I don't want my clothing back, but I do want you to have your own things while you're here," he explained. "And I thought today we could work more on the alphabet."

Calla had resisted his efforts to teach her to read thus far, finding it excessively difficult and preferring to draw. While he and Emmaline hadn't had children, Lucien suspected that was a common trait among people learning to read, regardless of age. That was how it started.

And he could read to her. He would have to find something interesting in the study he wouldn't use. He didn't mention any of that to Calla, though; instead, she shifted back to human form and dressed before he said goodbye and left for the village.

Edwin Hammond left him a map of the area, and Lucien stuck it in his pocket when he set out. He enjoyed the walk, only a couple of miles, and the first he'd taken since he arrived.

The map didn't even list a name for the village, but a faded painted sign announced it as Gull's End. There was almost nothing to see as Lucien trod through a tiny square ringed with shops and an inn, the latter of which had a painted sign advertising ready-made dry goods available inside. A pair of mismatched horses were tied outside the inn, and a man stood outside a butcher shop wearing a bloodstained apron, smoking a pipe. Rough dirt roads split off from the square, and houses of different sizes and styles dotted the landscape.

Lucien headed for the inn, and a bell over the door heralded his arrival. Despite the spring day's sunshine, it took a few seconds for his eyes to adjust to the darkness inside, thanks to the rows of shelves blocking two of the windows.

"Hello."

Lucien jumped before he saw the source of the voice. A silver-haired woman gave him a terse smile from behind the counter. "Good afternoon," he said. "I'm shopping for ready-made clothes today."

The smells of boiled potatoes and meat clung to the air, drifting in from another part of the building. There was probably a kitchen and dining area for the inn's patrons nearby. His nostrils constricted, and he was grateful he wasn't expected to subsist on any of that during his stay.

The clerk hopped down from her stool to join him on the other side of the counter. "We don't have the fancy ready-mades you're used to in London," she said. "But we have used clothing. Used good enough for you?"

The conversation had taken on more of a tense tone than Lucien expected from a small village shop. He was London-born and raised, and his accent reflected that. Still, he tried to be as amenable as he could make himself. "Of course," he said.

"Are you looking for trousers, waistcoats?"

"Ladies' attire, actually."

"Whatever for? You're all alone up there at Greaves Estate."

"I see word travels quickly," said Lucien. The village was so small that everyone knew each other; naturally, news of a stranger in town would get around. "And I'm not alone." His mind worked quickly, trying to think of how he could explain Calla's presence at the estate in the least scandalous way possible. "My cousin is staying with me," he explained. "She was able to visit me during my trip, and she didn't think she would be able to make it happen. Unfortunately, most of her baggage was misplaced during her journey." He pasted what he hoped was a friendly smile on his face. "Hence, my patronizing your shop today. She's rather exhausted after the whole ordeal."

The shopkeeper's look was inscrutable like she couldn't decide if she believed Lucien or not. "Ladies' attire is back here."

She led him to the back of the shop, where racks of clothes of yesteryear's fashions were displayed. "What'll your cousin need?" she asked.

"At least two complete changes of clothes," he replied. "Including undergarments."

That statement earned another look from the shop-keeper. Lucien fought the urge to smile; he didn't want to do anything to encourage her ire. Calla might find this funny when he told her.

"How big is she?" the shopkeeper barked. "For the corset and undergarments."

"About half a foot shorter than I am," replied Lucien. Calla was fairly tall, and he was exactly six feet. "She's slender."

"I have new undergarments for sale," she said shortly. "Do you know her measurements?"

He wondered if it would be gauche to show an estimation of Calla's waist measurement with his hands. "No. As I explained, she's quite slender."

The shop's proprietress opened a trunk pushed against the wall and removed a pair of traveling corsets, both in pristine condition, and sets of underwear. She thrust the clothes at Lucien and then dug through the racks of clothes. "What kind of dresses will she need?"

"Something for every day. She isn't especially fussy, as long as her clothing isn't mourning."

For some odd reason, that remark brought a tiny smile to the shopkeeper's face, and as Lucien took in the clothes available, he saw there was a remarkable number of black garments. "I have day dresses appropriate to the weather." She removed two dresses from a rack, one plain blue and the other pink and yellow striped. They were a few years out of fashion; even Lucien could tell that the dresses were meant to be worn with a bustle at some point and had been altered to remove some of the skirts' fabric. They were ugly but serviceable, and in a place like this, no one would care that Calla's clothing was out of date. Calla herself was unlikely to care, either.

"Thank you," Lucien said. "All of this will do nicely. I'll also need to bring her stockings and a pair of boots." It wouldn't be a bad idea for Calla to learn to walk while wearing footwear. "And a hairbrush," he added. "If you have one."

The proprietress carried the clothing to the counter and left it there, and Lucien did likewise with the undergarments she'd pushed at him. The suspicion she held in her gaze stood firm, and he had the distinct impression she didn't believe his story about his cousin visiting.

He didn't say anything, waiting for her to speak first, to tell him why she was being so odd.

"My husband's the caretaker at Greaves Estate," she finally said.

The knot of anxious nervousness he'd been holding on to dissipated a little. "Oh," Lucien said. "You know Mr. Hammond." He immediately felt like an idiot as soon as he said the words. *Of course, she would know Hammond.*

"Yes," she said. "Edwin said you're staying alone up there. He said you're a writer."

"I am, yes."

"Alone."

She arched an eyebrow so high it nearly disappeared into her hairline. Lucien tried not to sigh in irritation; being from London, he was unused to others prodding about his business as if they had the right. But he wasn't in London, and he would have to tolerate it now. "As I explained, my cousin is visiting," he said. "And she's short most of her belongings for the time being. In addition to the clothing, she's asked me to bring a hairbrush and pins, if you have them."

Perhaps something in his voice had given away his aggravation because she stopped her line of questioning. "A dry goods store has those things, even as remote as we are," she said brusquely. "And your cousin will want a light coat. It gets cold here at night, even in the spring."

Thus far, Calla seemed to be impervious to the cold, but Lucien didn't want to draw any more of the woman's ire. "Thank you," he said.

She stacked his purchases on the counter, and he already dreaded having to carry all of that back to Greaves Estate. He knew, without asking, that there was no way he would be able to finagle a carriage ride back to the estate, let alone the comfort of a steam cab. The packages were bulkier than he liked.

He spotted a box of Cadbury bars on the counter. *In for*

a penny, in for a pound. "And some of the chocolate, please," he said. He hoped his next phrase wouldn't be a lie, that Calla would like it. "It's my cousin's favorite."

❧

BACK IN THE HOUSE, dressed in her borrowed clothes and her hair roughly dried with a towel, Calla went to the kitchen for one of the sandwiches Lucien kept on hand for her. She'd need some strength for the next thing she had planned for the day: bowling.

Her arm still ached a little from lugging the ball around the first time she played, but she didn't care. There was an unexpected satisfaction to be found in pushing the ball down its polished lane just to knock something over. Calla hadn't known she had a destructive streak until she heard the crash of the pins for the first time.

She popped the last bite of sandwich in her mouth and cleaned up her plate the way Lucien did, thinking about how much she enjoyed scribbling across paper for no reason, either. Maybe that was an earlier hint of her appetite for destruction.

She leaned against the kitchen wall for a moment, rotating each ankle in turn until her feet felt—well, not quite normal. She wasn't sure she would ever get used to living on dry land, but her feet and legs felt less strained. Walking was coming easier to her more quickly than she expected, although her jaunts in the sea hadn't shown a decrease in her swimming skills.

A key scraped in the lock of the servants' exterior door. Her heart gave an unexpected flutter of excitement at the thought of seeing Lucien, and she smoothed her too-large shirt and smiled. *Why did I do that?*

She quickly answered her own question. *Because we're friends.*

She didn't have time to argue with herself over that unspoken statement when a short woman, older than Calla or Lucien, let herself into the house. Her hair was brown streaked with gray, pinned at the back of her head, and she held a huge wicker basket in her hands. If not for the fact that she was smiling, Calla might have tried to find a weapon.

"Oh, hello there!" the woman said. "I was expecting a gentleman, although I'm sure you're just as nice." She took off her bonnet and coat, draping them over hooks on the wall for such a purpose. "I'm Mrs. Claxton, but just call me Edna," she said warmly. "I'm the estate's cook. Pleased to meet you."

Calla wasn't entirely sure about manners in these kinds of situations; the humans she'd observed and occasionally spent time with tended to be rougher, less concerned with manners. She could blend in with them more easily in her human form.

She quickly glanced down at her bare feet and, above them, her rolled-up trouser cuffs.

There wasn't any way that she could have already made a worse first impression, and Edna Claxton still smiled at her.

"Hello, I'm Calla," she said.

Edna set about unpacking her basket, removing covered dishes. How did the small woman carry so much? "I was told there was only going to be one person here," she said, but her voice bore no trace of resentment at the presence of an additional guest. "It's a good thing I brought extra food," she added before Calla could say anything about her stay. "I'll still stop by tomorrow and leave more. I can't have you going hungry."

Calla relaxed a little, her shoulders slumping. "Your cooking has been appreciated," she said. "You're very good at it." Was that a suitable compliment?

Edna eyed her curiously as she removed a covered glass serving dish holding roasted meat of some kind. "Mr. Hammond told me Mr. Quinn was a widower," she said.

Calla nodded. "He is. I'm a friend. I'm visiting for a little bit before I move on."

"Where are you headed off to?"

"Scotland," she replied, but the name didn't hold the reverence for her it did before, now that she knew it wasn't as far away as she needed it to be.

"Where do you hail from?"

Fuck. Calla's brain grasped for a plausible answer and came up with none. She hadn't been made aware of her lack of knowledge about the world until a couple of days ago. She didn't sound like an Englishwoman, had no idea what she sounded like at all.

She said the first thing that came to mind. "Guess."

"Oh, you like games," Edna said. She opened a drawer and removed a carving knife. Calla felt her panic rise for a second until the cook began to slice the roast. "This heats up nicely on the stove if you're hard up for a hot meal," she said. "And as for guessing where you're from, I haven't the foggiest. Your accent's all over the map."

Her heart pounded so loudly she thought the cook might be able to hear it. "I'm from all over the map," she said, trying to sound lighthearted.

Edna barked out a laugh at that. "Oh, you like dirigibles and steamships, then? Can't say I've ever been on one myself." She tossed a critical eye on Calla's attire. "Why are you wearing men's clothes, honey? And where are your stockings and boots?"

She was saved when the servants' door opened again, and Lucien stepped inside.

Oh, thank the gods.

The thrill that coursed through her when she thought he'd arrived earlier returned.

He held large packages under each arm, and Calla quickly rushed to the doorway to help with them. He stared in shock at Edna. "This is the cook," Calla said. "Mrs. Edna Claxton. Edna, this is Lucien, who is renting the house."

"Charmed," said Lucien. He took away the package Calla was trying to finagle away from him and set it on the tiled floor with the other one. "Edwin Hammond told me you would be stopping by."

"I'm just refilling your cupboards," said Edna cheerfully. "Is the food to your liking?"

"Yes, it's been lovely." Lucien doffed his hat and coat, hanging them on a hook next to the cook's.

"Do you have any requests?"

Lucien glanced at Calla, probably thinking of the kinds of things she liked. "My cousin enjoys seafood," he said.

Edna laughed. "Prawns! Do you think I could get prawns any time soon?"

"No, but fish. I went to the village today, and I noticed a fishmonger's shop, but it was closed. Do you know its hours? I'm capable of preparing fish, especially on a stove as this one."

"Ah, a bachelor who isn't useless," said Edna. "Sadly, the fishmonger is a drunk and was likely sleeping off a bottle. It's hard to pin him down sometimes."

Lucien looked stricken at the mention of his being a bachelor, the affront to him and his late wife. "I'm widowed."

"Oh," said Edna demurred, as easily as if she'd been chatting about the weather. "My condolences."

She said those last words far too cheerfully for Calla's liking, and judging by the way Lucien's eyes narrowed, he thought so, too.

"My parents ensured I wasn't useless before I married, too," he added.

That statement seemed to catch Edna's attention, and her ever-present smile faltered. She quickly recovered and finished unpacking the food she'd brought. "I believe that's everything," she said. "I'll be back in two days, and I'll have extra food for your friend. All of this should keep you until then."

They said their goodbyes, and Edna put her hat and coat on before letting herself out.

The kitchen was silent for a few seconds. Calla and Lucien's eyes met, and she exhaled a sigh of relief she hadn't realized she was holding.

"She started off so pleasant," Calla said.

"She seems to be characteristic of everyone else I've met in this village," said Lucien. "Granted, that's only three people, but all of them have been a shade strange. And I'm rather odd, myself."

"She asked me where I was from, and I didn't know how to answer," Calla said. "I said everywhere."

"Which isn't a total lie," said Lucien. He hefted one of the packages, and Calla took the other one before he could. "I bought some clothes for you and a couple of other things." He cast a critical eye on Calla's package. "Will you be able to take that upstairs?"

"It isn't very heavy," she said. "And I've been practicing on the stairs." It wasn't as much fun as bowling would have been, but one of the last things she wanted to happen was tumble down the stairs and fracture something.

He looked dubious at hearing her claim but didn't argue with her.

She was slower than he was, but she made it to the landing with everything intact. They left the packages on Calla's bed, still unmade. She didn't see the point in making it look pretty when she was just going to mess it up again, anyway.

Lucien opened them. "They're not the most fashionable garments," he warned, holding open a box. Calla peeked inside to see a swath of blue fabric neatly folded. She lifted it out and held it up. It was a dress with a high neckline and puffed sleeves.

Maybe it'll look better in the looking glass.

She quickly crossed the room to the corner where the full-length looking glass stood and held the dress against herself. She tried not to show her disappointment.

But it was in vain. "It's terrible, isn't it?" said Lucien.

Calla draped the dress across the bed. "What were you thinking?"

"This was all the dry goods shop had," he explained. "There was absolutely nothing there that was made in the last decade. Many women in London wear trousers or waistcoats. They're more practical for those who work aboard steamships or dirigibles. But those fashions don't seem to have reached Gull's End. The only trousers the shop had were men's, and they were too large and dirty."

"What's Gull's End?"

"It's what the village has christened itself," Lucien said.

"I don't think I spotted a single gull during my time in the sea."

"Perhaps the 'End' part refers to their demise rather than a destination," said Lucien.

The idea was so ludicrous that it made Calla laugh. And the best part of that was Lucien did, too.

CHAPTER 7

*C*himes rang through the house, causing Lucien to drop his pencil on the ballroom floor. "What the devil?" he muttered.

Did the estate have a church bell he'd been uninformed of? He quickly ascended the ballroom's spiral staircase to the main floor, where he met Calla, who wore an equally confused look on her face.

"What was that?" she asked.

The chimes rang again, followed by a knocking at the door.

Lucien relaxed and put a hand on his chest, trying to calm down his rapidly beating heart. "I believe it's an especially odious version of a doorbell," he said.

She followed him as he weaved through the house's corridors, now as familiar to him as his own flat in London, before arriving at the front door. He hadn't been in the foyer since his arrival, preferring to use the servants' entrance in the kitchen. He threw open the door, no easy task considering its weight.

Edwin Hammond stood on the other side.

"Oh," said Lucien in surprise. "Mr. Hammond. Please come in."

Hammond stepped inside but made no move to remove his hat or coat. "Mr. Quinn," he said solemnly. He peered behind Lucien's shoulder. "Ah, my wife said you had company. I believe you met her today at the inn's shop."

Lucien quickly glanced over his shoulder at Calla, who lingered a few feet away from them. She gave the caretaker a hesitant wave. "Yes," Lucien said. "She only just arrived. And your wife is charming."

What a lie that was.

"How may I help you?" Lucien asked, wanting to know why the caretaker was here the same day Lucien ventured into Gull's End. "Mrs. Claxton has already been here."

"Yes, I spoke to her, too," said Hammond. "This also arrived at the post office for you." He removed an envelope from his pocket and held it out between two fingers at Lucien, who accepted it.

Good Lord, the man's acting like the post is cursed.

Lucien recognized the handwriting on the front as belonging to his editor at Cardwell Press, Peter Renton. He nodded and put the envelope in his trousers pocket, intending to read it later. "Thank you. Is all the mail to the estate directed to the village post office?"

"Yes. Although it wasn't the sole reason for my visit." The caretaker gave a pointed glance over Lucien's shoulder in Calla's direction.

"My cousin's arrival," said Lucien flatly. Irritation swamped him at just how invasive everyone involved in this house was. No one had given him a schedule as to when the cook or caretaker would be visiting. The proprietress of the dry goods shop seemed determined to be so unpleasant as to dissuade Lucien from ever returning. He saw, with perfect clarity, why the house's current owners refused to settle down and live here. Calling their neighbors odd was a tremendous understatement.

What the hell is wrong with Gull's End?

Hammond blinked at the sharpness in Lucien's tone. The caretaker had probably expected him to bend back over with apologies for having an extra person occupying the house. "There was nothing in my tenancy agreement that forbade houseguests," Lucien reminded him. "My cousin is in a spot of trouble in her travels and has decided to stay here for the time being."

"My wife said as much."

"And she's simply hanging about until she's ready to move on to the next part of her journey," Lucien added. He hoped his message could be read loud and clear without having to say it: Calla wasn't bothering anyone, nor was she damaging the property. Neither was Lucien, for that matter. Her staying with him didn't violate any contract he'd signed.

Hammond seemed to have picked up on the brusqueness and irritation in Lucien's voice, judging by the way he shrank back a little. Lucien was pleased to see that. "In that case," Hammond said, "I'd best be taking a quick tour of the grounds, just to ensure everything is as it should be."

"Please do," said Lucien. "And going forward, I would like you to keep to a schedule for these events. I would also ask you to pass on the message to Mrs. Claxton that she's to knock before entering the house. She nearly scared Calla half to death when she let herself in today."

Hammond nodded, but Lucien could tell from the set of his shoulders that he didn't care for his requests. "Has everything in the house been to your standards? Is there anything in need of repair?"

"No."

"I'll be checking on the greenhouse and boathouse, as well."

"The last time I looked at them, they were still standing." All of a sudden, Lucien remembered the boat and oars he'd borrowed the fateful night he met Calla. She'd brought back the boat, but the oars were somewhere on the seafloor.

Should he mention it? How could he explain their loss? Would it be easier to wait for Hammond to mention it and then pretend he knew nothing about it? Lucien had thrown his tenancy agreement into the caretaker's face, but there was bound to be a clause in there about missing property he couldn't think of at the moment.

Hammond gave him a tight-lipped smile and nodded. "I'm sure you would have mentioned it if the boathouse collapsed. I'll see to them and the gardens, in that case." He looked behind Lucien's shoulder and tipped his hat at Calla. "It was nice to meet your cousin."

Lucien was never so glad to see the back of the caretaker. He locked the door after Hammond left, leaning against it for a moment. He rubbed his eyes. "Does so little happen in Goose End that the residents have to be so strange?" he said.

"Gull's End," reminded Calla, joining him. Their upper arms touched, and this close to her, Lucien could again smell her hair. It was discomfiting and thrilling at the same time. He hadn't been close to anyone since Emmaline died.

"The arse of an annoying bird, anyway," said Lucien.

That remark made Calla laugh. "I like it when you curse. You should do it more often."

"Is cursing common in the mermaid kingdom?"

"Yes, and I'm not a mermaid princess," said Calla. "We don't have a royal structure like humans do."

"Only some humans recognize royalty."

"What of the ones who don't?"

"They're the sensible people," Lucien replied.

"I'm not sure mermaids are sensible, even though we don't have royalty," she said.

Lucien could sense the hesitancy in her voice; she wanted to tell him something but didn't know how. She had never told him the story behind her exile, and he didn't want to push it, just as she had never asked him for details about Emmaline. Part of him wanted to tell her everything, knowing she wouldn't think less of him or Emmaline's memory after he spilled out the entire sad tale, but he hadn't wanted to heap on her already considerable troubles. Nor did he want to go down the path of using Calla as a crutch for his problems.

He sneaked a glance at her. She had worried her lower lip between her teeth in a way that Lucien would have found alluring had her expression not been so tense.

"They exiled me," she finally blurted.

"I know," he said gently. "That was a terrible thing for them to do."

"Well, not entirely," she said. "I deserved it. I *think* I deserved it."

She said that last sentence with less conviction than she usually spoke with, and Lucien could only imagine how many hours she'd spent tormenting herself over being cut off from her life, her family, her friends.

He hadn't even thought to ask about her parents. Perhaps he fit right in with the village named after the arse-end of an annoying bird.

"What could you have possibly done that would have warranted exile?" he asked. "Did you kill anyone?"

That question earned a tiny shake of her head. Lucien could see the scars on her neck where her gills were cut, standing out in stark relief against her skin, and he fought the urge to shudder.

There was no sin she could have committed that would have justified the abuse she had endured under Isadore.

Lucien's hand balled into a fist of its own accord at the thought of Isadore. That was also a difficult subject they would have to discuss soon.

"Did you, I don't know, try to stage a coup?"

"No." But she smiled a little after he asked that. "No, nothing like that. I—I had a human lover." A blush bloomed on her face, and she looked away, blinking rapidly.

Of everything that went through Lucien's mind as to the reason for her exile, that possibility hadn't crossed it. "I see."

"I know your society doesn't care for those kinds of arrangements, too," she said. "And it isn't unusual for mermaids to do that. I just got caught."

Shame tinged her words, and Lucien's heart ached for her. "Calla," he began, but she kept speaking.

"I was curious," she said. "A harbor was the closest human settlement to us. I was always very careful, and until Isadore captured me, no one noticed me. I did spend some time on dry land. Once, I shifted at night, then stole a lady's dress from her garden. The clothes were left to dry there overnight, on a line."

Lucien nodded, absorbing this, the details of where she'd been before. A town or city with a harbor and an active shipping industry, which narrowed down the list of possible places where Isadore took her. "Where did you keep it?"

"I found a spot under a bridge to keep it dry," she said. "I found other bits of clothing, too. Boots, a hat. They weren't the nicest things, but they helped me blend in, and none of the humans there wore nice clothes, either.

"But none of that matters," she continued. "I met a nice sailor, and we met at a tavern a couple of times and spent a weekend together at its inn. I was curious about humans." She turned her head to face Lucien. "You look like you want to ask me something."

He did, but it was inappropriate and irrelevant to the story. "It's unimportant."

"You can ask me," she insisted. "I won't be offended."

"Your gills," Lucien said. "Did your companion not notice them?"

"'Companion,'" Calla said like she was tasting the word. "I like that. No, he didn't. Before Isadore got to me, when I shifted, my gills mostly disappeared. I would have had to point them out for someone to notice them."

Some of the tension in her melted away, evidenced by her leaning more of her weight against the door and Lucien. He didn't mind. Their odd area to have this conversation aside, he liked having this physical contact with her. It had been so long since another person touched him, even if he could only feel her body heat through his shirtsleeve.

"My people are quite permissive about physical relations," Calla said. "But only with other mermaids. That didn't keep plenty of us from seeking out humans for that reason, though.

"One of my former mermaid 'companions,'" she continued, emphasizing the word, "Spotted me in my human form on the last day of my lost weekend with the sailor and told our clan leader. I was exiled immediately."

Lucien was horrified. "How did your old lover see you on dry land? He was shifted in human form, wasn't he?"

Again, Calla nodded. "He wasn't kissing someone

goodbye in public. I was. I'd also been on land for two and a half days at that point, and they knew I was missing. We can fraternize with humans as long as we don't fuck them."

Lucien corrected her. "No, you can fuck humans as long as you don't get caught by a jealous ex-lover."

Her eyes widened in shock at his language.

"That was a reprehensible thing for him to do to you," he said. "And you did not deserve exile for that. I'm appalled. And our cultures have a lot more in common than not, at least when it comes to that area. That scenario has played out, over and over again, with human women, too. Calling it monumentally unfair doesn't adequately describe the injustice." His voice softened a little, trying to be reassuring. "How long have you been exiled?"

"Around two years," she said. "It's hard for me to keep track of the passing time sometimes while I'm alone."

"Do you know what year it is?" She'd been surprised to find out that Scotland wasn't as far away as she thought; Lucien didn't think it was a dumb question.

"Yes," she said. "We were guided by the human calendar in some ways. We mark the passing of seasons and years, although not in the kind of celebrations I've heard from the water from humans. You're quite fond of gunfire at night."

"No, we aren't." Lucien thought about what noises could be mistaken for gunfire underwater. "Perhaps you're thinking of fireworks displays."

"I don't know what that is. Only that they're very loud and shake the water."

"If the noise is marking holidays, it's likely fireworks," Lucien said. "They're created with gunpowder and a detonator." She wouldn't know what a detonator was, and Lucien barely understood them himself, so he added, "A device to make the gunpowder explode."

"Why the hells would you want to do that?" she asked.

"The gunpowder is mixed with colored pigments. The effect is very pretty," Lucien said.

Calla remained unconvinced.

His back was starting to protest its position against the door, and he straightened. The movement broke his contact, however small it was, with Calla, and he missed it immediately. "Do you want a drink?" he asked. "I think I could use a drink."

"I'd like that," Calla said.

There were bottles of spirits and glasses in the library and the study he didn't use, and he didn't feel like looking at shadow boxes of dead insects at the moment. He led her to the library instead. "Do you have a preference?" he asked, eyeing the collection.

"No."

He picked a bottle of Islay whiskey at random and poured two drinks. Calla busied herself with the globe that rested on a stand in the middle of the room. She spun it, fascinated, before accepting a glass from Lucien. "What's this?"

"The world as we know it. Here, hold out your glass before you drink from it."

She did so, and Lucien clinked his against hers. "What was that for?" she asked.

"It's a toast, albeit an informal one. They're made to mark an occasion." He took a generous sip from his glass.

"What's the occasion?"

He half-shrugged. "New friends, I suppose. Moving our lives forward in a positive way."

"I'm going to get as far away as I can from England," Calla said. "You're going to return to your home. Is that really moving forward?"

Lucien hadn't considered that. "Good point. My

writing is coming along for the first time in a very long time."

And while Emmaline's death still weighed on him, he'd felt… lighter, somehow, since he came to Greaves Estate. It wasn't entirely due to Calla's presence, although the change of scenery that he'd craved certainly played a part in that. He felt he'd finally turned a corner in his grief, a sign that his life could and would go on. That he might be capable of happiness again someday.

"You look like you want to say something," said Calla. She took a sip from her glass, and her expression shifted from curiosity to disgust. "Oh, that is *vile*."

Lucien hadn't spoken much about Emmaline with Calla, and he wasn't ready to dive into those details just yet. But she'd just opened up to him, telling him that she'd been expelled from her mermaid family for an unfair and ridiculous reason, and he knew she would listen and offer sympathy as far as his late wife was concerned.

"I was thinking that my life is going on," he said, echoing his thoughts. "And I'm pleased about that."

"You miss her," said Calla. It wasn't a question.

"Yes," said Lucien. He chose his next words carefully, struggling to coherently express his opinions on grief. "I mourned," he said. "Not only with wearing the black attire, although I did that, too. But after a while, I got used to her absence. And then I realized I didn't know who I was without her. Our marriage wasn't perfect, but we made it work, and I liked being her husband. I didn't know how much it tied into the rest of who I am until she died." He took a sip of his own drink, relishing the burn it cast down his throat. "I'm finding out who I am again. I'll still be that man when I go back to London."

He drained the rest of his glass. It wasn't the best way to appreciate an Islay whiskey, but he didn't care.

Calla was quiet, and she looked away from him to slowly turn the globe around on its axis with her free hand. She took another sip from her glass and barely made a disgusted face at the taste. "You loved her very much."

Her eyes met his, and he nodded.

He'd owed it to Emmaline to love her as much as he could. She'd sacrificed so much to be with him.

"Where's Scotland on this?" she asked.

He was grateful for the change in subject. Standing next to her, he spun the globe until he found Great Britain. The oceans and countries' boundaries were marked by different colors and shaped out of veined stone that Lucien couldn't identify, demarcated with brass fittings, and labeled with raised brass letters. "This is England," he said. He traced his finger a couple of inches north. "This is Scotland."

"But they're so close together!" said Calla, her voice nearly a wail.

"In the scheme of the entire planet, they are," Lucien said. "In terms of getting from here to there, not so much. The northernmost part of Scotland is hundreds of miles away. It would take days for you to swim there." He shifted the globe and pointed to continental Europe. "Perhaps there's a country here that would work for your escape, although the people don't speak English."

Calla looked more distraught than ever.

He moved the globe the other way. "English is spoken in North America. You'll need a passport to enter any of the countries, however."

"What's a passport?"

"A travel identity document," he replied. His own heart sank as he said the words. Calla would likely have a very difficult time procuring a passport.

She looked like she was ready to cry. "I can swim to

Scotland," she said. "I could swim here, too, couldn't I?" She pointed at France, the country carved from veined purple stone.

"I'm sure if anyone could swim across the English Channel, it would be you," Lucien said gently. "But English isn't spoken in France."

"What language is?"

"French."

"Do you speak it?"

"Poorly," he replied. "I can ask if someone speaks English, and if the answer is 'non,' I can ask if he knows someone who speaks English. I can order tea. That's it."

"Scotland," said Calla, more to herself. "I can still make it there."

An insane thought seized Lucien. "What about London? You could rent a room there," he said. "There aren't many places to swim. There's a river, but I would discourage you from even looking at it. It's filthy."

She bit her lip again in that enticing way he wasn't supposed to notice. She looked unconvinced. "It's a very large city," he said. "Isadore would never be able to find you."

There was a selfish part of him that was encouraging these suggestions. She was the first friend he'd made since Emmaline died. He didn't want to run the risk of never seeing her again.

"May I consider it?" she finally said. "I still think I'd like to go here." She pointed to the northernmost part of Scotland on the globe. It wasn't specifically demarcated, but Lucien recognized it as the Shetland Islands. "Isadore can't touch me if I'm in the open water, away from a harbor."

Sadness wrapped a cold hand around Lucien's heart,

but he nodded anyway. "It's your decision to make. I'll help you, no matter what."

"Mr. Quinn."

Hammond's disapproving voice had both of them lifting their gazes from the globe. The sadness he'd been feeling at the thought of Calla's departure was replaced by anxiety. How much of their conversation had the caretaker heard?

Before Lucien spoke, Hammond said, "I inspected the boathouse."

Ah, yes, the oars. The caretaker had noticed their absence. Lucien decided to take the cowardly path and pretend he'd never set foot in the boathouse. He schooled his features into what he hoped was a neutral expression. "Is everything all right in the boathouse?"

"No," replied Hammond. "A pair of oars is missing. They were hanging on the wall on hooks. Have you seen them?"

Lucien shook his head. "I haven't set foot in the boathouse since you escorted me on a tour of the property."

Hammond looked like he didn't believe him. "Are you certain?"

"Extremely," replied Lucien.

The caretaker glared at him and Calla in turn. Calla shifted on her bare feet and looked down at the globe again.

"Because the oars disappeared during your tenancy, you are responsible for its replacement," Hammond said. "I will be informing Mr. Greaves about its loss, and I will be submitting an invoice to you."

"Understood."

Hammond gave him another suspicious glance. Lucien returned it.

"I'll be back for another inspection in a few days," Hammond finally said, breaking the silence. "Miss... I didn't get your name."

Calla looked at Lucien, flummoxed. "Quinn," she blurted out.

"Miss Quinn," Hammond said. "Delighted to meet you." He sounded anything but. "Mr. Quinn, take care. And take care of this estate."

"I'll see you out," said Lucien. He set his empty glass down on the globe's hammered brass stand, and with a quick look at Calla, followed the caretaker to the foyer.

CHAPTER 8

*S*unlight filtered through the bedroom's curtains, waking Calla.

She had slept better than she ever had since Lucien took her in. But it remained a mystery whether her improved rest was due to her very comfortable human bed or feeling safe at last.

Perhaps it was because she felt like she belonged somewhere for the first time since she was exiled.

It was Lucien, too. His offer of moving to London was a temptation; the only things that kept her from accepting were his warning of filthy rivers and the prospect of staying in a rented room without him.

She had no idea how to care for herself on dry land, and seeing the globe the day before was a stark reminder of how little she truly knew. Swimming to a remote part of Scotland, staying underwater, was the safest thing for her to do. It was for Lucien, too. She didn't want to attract Isadore to him.

She reluctantly got out of bed, already missing the

warmth of the blankets. And then stared down a new enemy, waiting for her in the wardrobe against the wall.

Her new clothing.

As much as she preferred to keep wearing men's attire for the sake of convenience and comfort, she knew Lucien needed his clothes back. And if Mr. Hammond or Mrs. Claxton or any of the other sour-faced citizens of Gull's End stopped by the house and saw her, she needed to remain as inconspicuous as possible. So, ladies' clothes it meant.

She quickly washed her face and dragged the brush he'd given her through her hair, wincing as it pulled on the knots there. She opened the wardrobe door and removed plain, bright white undergarments and a corset. She hadn't bothered with a corset during her jaunt with the sailor, and the women she saw around the tavern and inn they'd stayed in didn't appear fussed about them. But outside of taverns, they were expected. It was vitally important that she blend in.

She stripped off Lucien's shirt, the same one she wore the day before and to bed. She'd done it for his sake more than hers; she was used to being naked. Just as she was doing this for his sake now.

She put on the undergarments, then held up the corset to herself. "Here goes," she whispered.

She unhooked the front and put it around herself and re-hooked it, fingers occasionally stumbling over the tiny metal eyes. Doing so was far more tedious than she expected it to be.

The corset sagged around her, defeating its purpose. Lucien had explained the day before how it was supposed to fit, that the laces on the back needed to be tightened.

She'd forgotten that part. She sighed, unhooked it, set the garment on the bed, and studied it. She pulled the laces tighter and tied their ends in a bow, then tried to put it on again.

Now it was too small.

"Fuck!" she snapped and threw it on the bed.

A gentle rapping at the door startled her. "Calla?" said Lucien from the other side. "Is everything all right?"

She opened the door to see him, sandy hair disheveled, wearing a belted robe and a sleepy, confused expression.

She'd never seen him undressed before, and she felt herself blush. "Everything's fine," she said. Just as quickly, she corrected herself. "Well, not entirely. I'm having trouble getting dressed."

He blinked, then his eyes widened in understanding. He peeked behind her to take in the sight of the corset on the bed. "Oh."

"I need some help," she said. "I have to learn to wear them, don't I?"

"I—yes," he said. He looked away from her for a second at something in the corridor before he stepped into the room.

Calla looked down at the yards of her undergarments. "I can get the easy clothes on without a problem," she said. "I just didn't know how to make the corset work."

He picked it up and unlaced it. "I'll help you get into this," he said. "And then you can simply unhook the front of it later. Leave it as it is, and it'll hold its shape for the next time you wear it. Turn around."

Even though he only just awakened, there was a quiet authority to his voice that commanded Calla's attention. Wordlessly, she turned around to face away from him.

"Hold out your arms," he said.

She did so.

Lucien wrapped the front part of her corset around her, fitting it around her body. "Take a deep breath."

Calla obeyed.

Then he said something unexpected. "I apologize," he said, his breath ruffling her hair. "This won't be the most comfortable."

He tightened the laces, the sound of ribbons threading and pulling against the garment's metal eyes the only noise in the room. It took a couple of seconds for her to realize how much tighter it was becoming, how she could already feel her freedom of movement being restricted.

Warring feelings emerged in her: the prickles of awareness as her nerves lit up, ignited by Lucien's nearness and both of their states of undress, fighting with the unfamiliar and unwelcome sensation of constriction.

Lucien's deft fingers finished lacing the corset, and she felt her hair puff around her shoulders as he tied the ribbons in a bow. "You've had practice with that," Calla said.

His breath hitched behind her, and she wondered if she'd said the wrong thing.

Of course you did. Remember his wife, idiot.

But he surprised her when he put his hands on her shoulders and urged her to turn around. The first thing she noticed was how warm he was through the flimsy fabric straps of her underdress, whatever it was called.

"I'm a quick learner," he said simply.

Before she could contemplate the meaning behind those words, he nodded at the open wardrobe. "Do you need some help with a dress?"

Neither of them had fastenings or buttons on the back, so Calla would be able to manage them on her own. "I'll be fine," she said. "Thank you."

He gave her a smile before leaving the room. "I'll see you at breakfast," he called from the corridor.

~

As LUCIEN SET about toasting bread and poaching eggs for breakfast, he wondered what the hell had come over him.

He didn't know which part of his encounter with Calla was the most inappropriate: offering to help her dress, lacing her up, touching her, or his own thoughts about her. He tried to reason it away: he'd heard her swearing and investigated, totally forgetting in his sleepy, early morning fog that Calla cursed a lot for reasons he didn't out loud.

She hadn't known how to put on a corset herself. Most women started wearing them when they were still children.

He prepared a pot of tea, and as its fragrant steam wafted through its spout, he realized what needled him the most.

It was Calla's remark about his having laced corsets before. It wasn't the speaker or her words; it was his reaction to them.

He hadn't thought of Emmaline at all. And Emmaline was the last person he'd laced into a corset. The last person whose corset he'd unlaced, too.

No, all he could think about in those moments was Calla: the way she looked first thing in the morning, her long dark hair curling at the ends. How the sunlight filtering through the curtains highlighted the outline of her body in its pristine white undergarment, the sight of which nearly left him tongue-tied. It shouldn't; he'd seen her nude or nearly so repeatedly in the days since they met. He'd been so flustered he hadn't even pointed out that she hadn't had on stockings.

She was beautiful, and for the first time in a very long time, he was attracted to someone. It was disconcerting and not because of loyalty to Emmaline's memory. Calla depended on him. She needed him to navigate her way on dry land.

He heard the pad of her bare feet on the floor behind him and turned around.

Calla had combed her hair but left it loose, a startling and alluring contrast to the uncomfortable formality of the attire he'd picked out for her. She smiled gamely at him, but he could tell from the pained expression on her face that she was uncomfortable.

"I hope you're hungry," he said.

She tugged on the tightly buttoned collar of her dress. "Always."

He set their food on a tray and carried it to the dining room, where they took their usual seats. Calla poured tea for each of them, and after taking a sip, said, "The hell with this."

"I beg your pardon?"

Her dark eyes met his, and she unfastened the top buttons of her dress.

Lucien nearly dropped his teacup. It wouldn't have been the first time where she was concerned.

But she stopped as soon as the top buttons were undone. She sighed or tried to. "That's a little better," she said and cut into her eggs and toast. As soon as she swallowed her first mouthful, she said, "I don't want you to think I'm ungrateful, but I don't care for these clothes quite yet."

She'd chosen the plain blue dress, and while the design left something to be desired, she looked lovely in blue. "I think you look lovely," Lucien said.

Calla's hand, still holding her fork, paused in mid-air. He wondered if he'd made a gaffe.

"Is it because I look like a proper lady now?" she asked.

Very little about her appearance could be construed as

proper, from her unbound hair to her bare feet, to the open collar at her throat. "No," he said. "You don't. And that's one of the things I like about you. The color suits you, is all."

Color touched her cheeks, and she gave him a shy smile in response. "Thank you."

They ate in silence for a few moments until she asked, "What did Mr. Hammond give you yesterday?"

Lucien stilled, searching his memory of the day before, but all he recalled was leaning against the front door with her while she poured out her past to him.

And Edwin Hammond had delivered a letter, addressed to him in his editor's handwriting.

"Damn," he muttered.

He nearly vaulted himself out of his seat in a mad rush to his bedroom to find the clothes he had worn the day before. Dimly, he heard Calla's voice as she trailed behind him. "Lucien?" she called from the bottom of the stairs. "Is everything all right?"

He found the envelope, slightly crushed, in his trousers pocket in the laundry basket. Clutching it in his hand, he retraced his steps to the landing and walked down the stairs more carefully.

Calla waited for him at the foot, a worried look on her face. "Did I make you forget something important?" she asked.

He'd forgotten, but it wasn't her fault. "No," he said. He tore open the envelope and removed the letter inside.

Peter Fenton, the lead editor at Cardwell Press, possessed the impeccable penmanship that only a man in publishing could have. As soon as he remembered the envelope, Lucien had been terrified that the letter contained a notice terminating his contract for failure to produce, but he was mercifully, pleasantly surprised.

Fenton only wanted an update as to his newest book as soon as possible.

"What does it say?" Calla asked. Then, "Is it polite to ask that?"

"With me, always." He read the letter's contents aloud to her. "I'll have to send a response right away. I'll have to take another trip into the village to see if the post office has a telegraph machine." He silently berated himself for not checking the last time he was there and could only hope the postmaster wasn't as unpleasant as the rest of the village citizenry.

"Can I come, too?" There was a hopeful note in Calla's voice.

Part of Lucien desperately wanted to say yes, to show her more of the elements of his world, and to take the opportunity to be near her for as long as he could be.

But a more practical part of him looked at her bare feet and remembered that she was unused to walking in boots, let alone walking in them along a rutted dirt road, even if the distance was only a couple of miles.

He hated to disappoint her. "I don't think that's a good idea," he said gently. "It's too far when you aren't used to wearing boots or shoes."

Her face fell but picked up just as quickly. "I'll bowl, then."

The practical part of Lucien reared its head again, urging him to remind her to practice her letters. But he didn't want to nag her, not when she looked so happy right now.

For some strange reason, bowling made his mermaid happy.

No, not your *mermaid.*

Good Lord, he'd helped her into her clothes *once*, and his body thought he should have designs on her.

"That sounds fine," Lucien replied.

~

With Lucien gone to the village, Calla once again found herself alone, staring down the length of the estate's bowling lane.

She rotated her ankles, one at a time, then took a deep breath. Or tried to. The stupid corset impeded that quite a bit. Then she hefted the bowling ball and set it rolling.

By all the gods of the land and sea, she was going to knock down all the pins in one roll again.

She held her breath as the ball rolled toward the end of the lane, willing it to stay on the straight course she hoped she'd plotted.

It veered to the left. "Fuck," muttered Calla.

Its impact knocked down all but one of the pins. "Fuck!" she said again, louder this time, her voice bouncing off the room's walls.

She reset the pins and fetched the ball. Once again, she sent it rushing down the lane, breath held.

Two pins remained standing after the ball hit them.

Irritation welled in her. She couldn't even draw her arm all the way back in these stupid clothes. She didn't think her poor bowling performance was entirely due to her aim or her strength, both of which were improving.

Fuck it. I'm alone for the time being, and I'll never be a lady, anyway.

Calla set about unfastening the row of tiny buttons that marched down the front of her dress and pulled it over her head. The stupid corset went next, unhooked as quickly as her fingers could do so. The dress was draped over the room's open door of the closet where the ball and spare pins were stored, the corset unceremoniously tossed to the floor.

Calla finally took in a deep, unfettered breath. *Thank all the gods.*

Once again, she reset the pins and retrieved the ball. She returned to her starting position and raised the ball, targeting the pins in her line of sight.

She pulled her arm back, moved it forward a few inches, and let the ball fly.

Finally, every single pin was knocked down.

She was sure her shriek of delight could be heard all the way in Gull's End. She wished Lucien was here to see it.

She took a few seconds to admire the mass of fallen pins, then took off to reset them and retrieve the ball.

Calla didn't know how much time passed as she played, only that she hit all of the pins at once three more times as she did. She couldn't remember the last time she'd had so much fun just for the sake of it. Certainly before she was exiled.

She pushed away those ugly memories threatening to resurface and focused on her game.

By the time the sun was as high in the sky as it could get, she heard familiar footsteps in the corridor and smiled. She held the ball aloft, with a set of upright pins at the opposite end of the lane. Hopefully, with Lucien watching, she could hit all of them again.

He appeared in the doorway, pink-cheeked from his walk to and from Gull's End. He had a smile on his face at first, but it quickly gave way to shock.

Then Calla remembered she was undressed. Again.

She pretended she'd forgotten. "Watch this," she said happily and sent the ball soaring across the polished floor.

Please, please all fall down.

The gods were smiling on her because every pin collapsed to the floor. "That isn't even the first time I did it!" she crowed. She scampered down the lane to right the pins.

Lucien's surprise had faded away, and he smiled. "I believe that's called a strike, although it's been a fair amount of time since I last played. And when I did, it was bad."

"You were drunk as a lord, weren't you?"

"I had my fair share of port that night, yes."

Calla picked up the ball and returned to the opposite end of the lane. "Want to try again?"

"I did, the other night. And my performance was poor."

She held out the ball in his direction. Her arms shook a little with the weight of it. "Just this once."

He didn't protest but crossed the short distance between them and took it from her hands.

"If I knock over at least three pins, we'll work on your reading this afternoon," he said.

"And if you don't?"

Lucien clearly hadn't considered that. "I can usually knock over three."

"But if you *don't* knock over three pins this time?" she pressed. "What if I don't feel like studying the alphabet today?" Her tongue deliberated, nearly stumbled over the word "alphabet." It still sounded strange to her ears, like it was a word in another language. It was clunky, even when Lucien and his smooth voice and accent said it.

"What do you want?"

Was it Calla's imagination, or was there a husky note to his voice—his *smooth* voice, she reminded herself—that wasn't there before? She nearly said, "A kiss," but stopped herself in time.

He had insinuated he was her protector and friend, not a lover.

He still grieved his late wife.

At the very least, such a suggestion was incredibly manipulative.

She decided it must have been her imagination. "We go swimming," she said. "Or I'll swim, and you can splash around where the water isn't too deep."

He stared at her, aghast. "Are you mad?"

"Of course not. I swim all the time."

"You're built for it!" he said, still incredulous at the suggestion. For a couple of seconds, she was worried he might say something about her being half-fish, and if he did, she might cry. She was *not* part animal. Just a shifter and a woman.

"It's autumn!" he continued. "I'll freeze!" He shifted the ball's position in his hands. Calla couldn't help but notice that his arms didn't tremble at all at its weight.

"Just for a few moments," she said. "And a night swim will only happen if you don't hit at least the three pins you claim you can knock over."

"What the devil? You're adding to my sentence. A *night* swim?"

The look on his face was too much, and Calla laughed. "Only if you can't do it."

"The hell I can't," said Lucien. Under his breath, he muttered, "There is no bloody way I'm getting in that water at night ever again."

"What about during the daytime?"

Lucien was trying to angle the ball to line up with the center pin. "Stop trying to distract me."

Calls hadn't intended to distract him, just tease him, but she had changed her aim.

Without taking his eyes off the ball, he said, "I might consider a swim in the summertime. If the water's nice."

"We may have different opinions on 'nice' water."

"I'm sure you're impervious to cold," he said. He took his eyes off the ball and lane for a second to slant a glance at her.

"I don't know what 'impervious' means," she said. "And would you throw the ball?"

"In this case, it means you're not bothered by the cold," he replied. "It also means you're waterproofed, I suppose, so it's an appropriate word to use either way. Your physiology is better suited to cold water than mine is. And I will *not* throw the ball. Edwin Hammond was nearly apoplectic about missing oars. Could you imagine what he would do if I left a bowling ball-shaped hole in the floor? Because that's what happens when a bowling ball is thrown."

"Gods in all the seas!" roared Calla. "Just let go of the fucking ball already!"

His arms shook with laughter, and he nearly dropped the ball. As it was, he sat down at the end of the lane, the ball beside him. Calla, not knowing what else to do, did likewise.

"You could sit down on the floor and push it," she suggested. "You might get the ball's path straight if you did that."

"Good Lord." He gave a beleaguered, exaggerated sigh and rose to his feet. The mischievous smile he'd shown her before and that she was starting to love returned, and she stepped back, waiting.

He pulled his arm back, waited half a second, and pushed it forward. The ball hit the floor with a small thud and rolled faster than she'd ever seen from him to crash into the pins.

One remained standing.

"Damn it," said Calla, but she wasn't that irritated about the alphabet lesson. Reading was a vitally important skill she would have to have to navigate this new world on land, difficult as it was to acquire.

And at least that meant she would spend more time cozied up to Lucien. Or as cozied up as one could get in chairs next to each other, in an orchestra pit in a strange, subterranean ballroom.

Lucien gave her a triumphant smile. She wanted to kiss it off him but refrained from doing so. Instead, she said, "Next time, I'll win the wager, and you'll swim with me in the sea."

"I hope to God it won't be before the summer," he said. "Not that I expect the sea to be much warmer then."

Irrational hope flared in Calla at the mention of the following summer.

Perhaps he would visit her in Scotland when she finally made it there.

But the thought of settling there no longer held the allure it did before she met him. The thought of leaving him behind made her incredibly sad.

She didn't mention Scotland; she didn't even want to think of it at the moment. So, she said, "You won. Let's start that reading lesson."

CHAPTER 9

*C*alla had picked up the alphabet and basic phonetics within a remarkably short period of time. A few days after Lucien insisted on her having regular reading lessons, she could identify every letter of the alphabet and sound out short words. She could spell her own name without being prompted, and after a couple of tries, Lucien's as well. Her penmanship wasn't the strongest, but that would come in time.

The following Sunday had them waking up to freezing cold rain, characteristic of this part of the country in early October. Or any part of England, Lucien thought.

Winter was on its way and making its impending arrival known.

Even Calla, as used to the cold as she was, was unsure about taking her daily swim. "Are you getting soft on land?" Lucien teased her over their morning tea.

"I could be," she replied. "There's a lot to like about land." She drained the last of her cup and returned it to its saucer with an unladylike slam and leaned back in her chair. The top buttons of her dress were unfastened per usual, and since the day he found her bowling in her underwear, she'd stopped wearing a corset.

She was willing to make sacrifices for living in relative safety among humans, she'd said, but wearing what she called a cage wasn't one of them.

Her dresses didn't drape correctly without the garment, but neither she nor Lucien cared. Privately, he liked how she dressed carelessly, with her comfort at the forefront of her mind. There was a raw sensuality there, too, that hadn't escaped his notice.

Her voice snapped him back to reality, and he put aside his lascivious thoughts about his charge. "Speaking of land, we should look at a map today," she said. "You said before we might be able to figure out where I came from and where Isadore could be."

"Excellent idea."

"As long as I'm not interfering with your writing," she added quickly. "I know your new book is important."

He'd been making incredible headway on his new novel, but if even if he hadn't, he still would have preferred to spend the day with her, poring over a map. "It's the day of rest," he said. "I can take a break from the book." In fact, it would do him some good.

"You'll have to read to me from it someday," said Calla. She stood up and collected their dishes, and he followed her from the dining room to the kitchen.

"Do you think you would be interested in a novel about a downed dirigible's passengers stranded on an island? It might put you off flight travel."

She shrugged. "Your stories are all made up. I'm not afraid of make believe."

They had a good system set up: Lucien would wash, Calla dry and put away. She'd tried washing the dishes once but found that the water caused the remains of her gills to activate themselves, which she explained was uncomfortable.

The only room in the house that had maps was the study. He'd avoided it as much as he could, only stopping in there occasionally for more paper or to search it for some colored pencils, which he'd given to Calla. But as the two of them walked in and started poking around the shelves and desk for a detailed map of the country, he realized the room didn't have the hold on him he thought it did.

So there were insects and butterflies behind glass in there, pierced through their bellies with dressmakers' pins in straight rows. And Emmaline would have liked them, with her taste that bordered on the macabre. Lucien didn't, and he didn't have to. They were only bugs, probably arranged in their shadow boxes like trophies by a long-ago child in the Greaves family.

Emmaline had never been here. Lucien wasn't disrespecting her memory by inhabiting this space, nor was he doing so when he left their London flat. She hadn't cared for it in the last couple years of their marriage, anyway.

"Lucien."

Calla's voice was insistent as if she'd tried and failed to get his attention already. Perhaps she already had. She held out a rolled-up map. "This is what we're looking for, isn't it? This is what maps look like on shipwrecks."

"And it is indeed a map," said Lucien, accepting the roll. He unfurled it to reveal a map of Great Britain and Ireland. "This is perfect."

The secretary was too small for the map to be spread out and both of them to hover over it. It wasn't as though Calla would be inconvenienced by sitting on the floor anyway, given her lack of a corset and petticoats.

He would *never* stop noticing that.

"Our goal is to guess where Isadore's likeliest location is," he said. "I believe you mentioned you were captured from the water."

She nodded. "There was a big harbor," she said. "Probably more than one. There were a lot of ships and sailors."

"What did they sound like?"

"Not like you," she said.

"What about Hammond or Mrs. Claxton?" he asked. Both of them bore strong accents, but they were different. Hammond's spoke of a lifetime spent in and around Manchester, and Mrs. Claxton's had a distinctive Yorkshire bite to it.

She shook her head and stared at the map before her as if willing it to tell her what she wanted to hear.

Lucien was still encouraged. "So, this means we can cross Manchester off our list," he said. "There are a few other port cities worth our consideration, though." London was the epicenter of massive transportation hubs, and its hodge-podge of accents would make finding Isadore very difficult.

But Lucien didn't think that was where Isadore was. London's waterfront faced the river, and Calla had been traveling in the sea. Additionally, the Thames was filthy and frequented by any number of boats and people. Calla would have been noticed.

Just to be sure, he asked, "What was the water like? Clean, dirty?"

She tilted her head to the side, thinking. "Well, dirty. Harbors always are. The harbor led out to the sea, and I remember swimming in a straight line away from my people after I was exiled." She paused. "At least, I *think* it was a straight line. My navigation skills haven't been the same since Isadore took me."

Now it was Lucien's time to still. "A straight line?"

She nodded.

That provided the biggest clue yet. "Liverpool," Lucien said. "Isadore took you from a Liverpool harbor." He pointed to the spot on the map. "And your people have situated themselves off the Dublin coast." He pointed to the Irish capital with a finger on his other hand. Just to be sure, he asked, "What were the accents like among those sailors closest to your home?"

"Stronger," she replied. "If that makes sense. When some of them spoke, it was almost a whole other language, even though they were speaking English. I did hear a lot of familiar English accents, though. Like yours."

"And you *sure* you swam straight across?"

The look she gave him clearly said she questioned his intelligence, but she nodded. "I know those waters better than the ones here."

Even though he'd known Calla for a while now and had seen her in her mermaid form several times, it was still shocking to know that a colony of mermaids lived in the Irish Sea, undisturbed. "Fascinating," he murmured.

"That I know the waters? Wouldn't it be the same with you knowing London's roads?"

"I suppose so."

She leaned forward a few inches until he could see every fleck of gold in her big, dark eyes. "I'm sure you could blindfold yourself and wander through London, and you would know where you are just by the scents and the feel of the ground under your feet."

She was right.

"I would," he said. "I think I would know every area I've ever lived in if I was blindfolded. And a few more that I haven't because they made such an impression on me."

"How so?"

"The memories of the places my father brought me to," he replied. "I wasn't raised in abject poverty, but my father did, and he brought me to North Kensington on a couple of occasions to show me where he grew up. I'll never forget how the neighborhood smelled." At her quizzical look, he explained, "It's a slum. My father did well enough for himself, and when he married my mother, they lived in a perfectly average flat in Chelsea. I was raised there." He paused. "I apologize. You asked about walking around London blindfolded, and I'm babbling."

"I'm learning more about you, so I don't mind," Calla said. "You told me once your mother was from France?"

"She came to England as a child, but she kept the language. My grandmother named me." That wasn't the point of the story, which had already veered off. "My father took me to his former neighborhood, and I think it was to show me how easily one's life can unravel. His father was a blacksmith and lost his shop, and the family settled there. When my grandfather died, my father stayed there with his sisters and mother.

"Father and Maman did well enough for themselves," Lucien continued. "But they always wanted me to remember how things can shift on a whim. It's a lot easier to fall down than to keep yourself standing up. One of my mother's ancestors was a minor noble and beheaded during the Terror."

"What's the Terror?"

"France did away with their monarchy," Lucien said. "And that's the polite explanation." Curiosity had her brows arching nearly to her hairline, so he added, "The people spoke and acted. Many were executed."

"Hm," said Calla. She adjusted her position, tucking her knees under her. "I thought my fellow mermaids were cruel."

"Humans are among the most unevolved creatures on the planet."

She nodded, and he wondered if she was thinking of Isadore.

A crack of thunder boomed, not unlike the one he'd heard the night he met Calla. The rain intensified, droplets throwing themselves against the windows.

"May I ask you something?" Calla sounded shy. "And I'll understand if you don't want to answer. But we've shared so much, and if you don't want to, please don't get angry with me."

"I don't think I *could* get angry with you."

"What happened to Emmaline?"

Calla folded her hands in her lap, an innocent gesture that belied the gravity of her question. But Lucien knew her well enough to see the fine tremor in her fingers. She was nervous.

She shouldn't be. He'd wanted to tell someone about Emmaline for so long.

He had wanted to tell Calla about her but didn't know how.

When he didn't respond right away, Calla said, "I'm sorry."

"No," he said quickly. "Don't be. I'll tell you."

"Do you need a drink first?" She inclined her head to the cabinet where the estate's whiskey was stored.

He shook his head. "I'd rather be sober, but thank you. Perhaps after the story's finished."

He leaned back and stretched out his legs, trying to put everything that had happened into words. It wasn't just Emmaline's death he was going to tell Calla about, but how their marriage came to be.

"As I told you, I grew up middle class," Lucien said. "My father founded a company that sold brass fittings and fixtures. We weren't wealthy but comfortable enough. My mother didn't have to work, and I was sent to decent schools. My uncle took over the business after Father passed, and it's still doing well.

"We were excluded from upper-class society, of course," Lucien continued. "Not that my parents cared about that kind of thing. Some people in trade have managed to infiltrate their ranks, but they're not equal, not really. My father conducted business with some titled people, but he never exposed me to their world. I found out later that it was also due to my mother being French. It's a fine thing to hire a French chef but another altogether to marry and have a son with a Frenchwoman."

"But you said she came to England as a girl."

"She did, but she had a French name—Adrienne—and still occasionally spoke French with me at home. She lowered herself to speak it with the French servants they employed. That simply isn't done.

"I knew early on that the life of an entrepreneur wasn't for me," Lucien continued. "My father understood and sent me to university, which is why his brother now controls the business. I'm still entitled to a percentage of its profits." That money had kept him afloat during the dark months following Emmaline's death when he couldn't write worth a damn.

"Emmaline came from a more prosperous family," he said. "They made their fortunes through a combination of trade and strategic marriages. Our fathers were business associates, and we met, by chance, at my family's home when I was home for the Christmas holidays in my final year of university."

He could still clearly recall those first heady days of wonder when he realized he'd met the woman he wanted to marry. He'd known before Emmaline did.

"Emmaline was supposed to marry a viscount," Lucien said. "He was at least twenty years older than she was and in need of an heir. Her parents wanted the respectability that such a marriage would bring them."

"But she married you," said Calla softly. He had the sense that she guessed where this story was going.

"To her family's everlasting ire," Lucien confirmed. "Her parents cut her off. We had a small ceremony the winter after I graduated and were very happy for a few years. I established myself as an author, and my royalties and the percentage of profits from my father's company brought in a decent living for us."

He still lived in the same Portman Square flat he'd shared with Emmaline. It hadn't felt like home since she died; the thought that he made this trip in the first place meant his subconscious wanted him to move house.

Calla didn't say anything, instead fixing her gaze on him as she waited for him to continue.

"I couldn't provide her with the fineries she enjoyed before we married," he said. "We didn't attend the types of events she used to enjoy, and we didn't receive any invitations." He quickly corrected himself. "Well, *she* didn't receive any invitations. I never did in the first place. I was beneath her station."

A shadow seemed to have cast itself over Calla's face, and she finally spoke with an uncharacteristic tenderness in her voice. "Oh, Lucien, you aren't beneath anyone."

He was touched by her concern. "That's very kind of you to say, but that isn't how London society viewed us," Lucien said. "And that was all right for her, for the first few years."

"Until it wasn't," said Calla knowingly.

Lucien supposed Calla's guess about his relationship with his wife was correct. "The last two years were very difficult," he said. "She missed her old life, and she started voicing doubts about her decision to marry me instead of going forward with the marriage her parents tried to arrange. She claimed that believing in love was a mistake, and if she could do everything over again, she would have chosen the viscount. She was angry to be saddled with a writer."

Something flashed in Calla's eyes, dark and angry, but he forged on.

"She threatened me with a divorce," he said. "I begged her to reconsider, and she did. We seemed to have come to an understanding and made up a few months before she got sick."

Another peal of thunder sounded, followed by a bright flash of lightning in the windows. "How did she get sick?" Calla asked quietly.

"Influenza. It was a particularly bad year for it, all through London. We both contracted it." Lucien's voice softened as he remembered how Emmaline's strength kept waning as his returned. "No one ever thinks something as innocuous as a cough and sniffling nose can lead to something that kills."

He picked at a loose thread on his trousers. "Everyone gets them every winter, and they're brushed away with some hot tea and fresh air. But...not for Emmaline."

She was twenty-seven when she died, a year younger than Lucien, and had been the picture of health before she came down with that cough.

Neither of them spoke for a few moments, the only sound that of the rain.

"It's a bit anticlimactic, isn't it?" Lucien finally said. "Influenza is the most ordinary of deaths, but we carry on behaving and grieving as if our loved ones died valiantly in a war."

Calla put a proprietary hand on his arm, and he realized he was shaking. "Lucien."

"Humans judge others' right to grieve based on how one died. Influenza, childbirth, industrial accidents—they're considered unimportant deaths."

"*Lucien*." Calla's tone grew a little more insistent.

"They're justified as necessary more often than you would expect. It's absolutely vile that one's chance at surviving those incidents usually comes down to having the funds to pay a doctor for help. It's so unfair that someone should get a better or renewed chance at life simply by virtue of being born into a station in life they had nothing to do with." A ragged breath escaped him. "And Emmaline was born into it. She gave up that station when she married me."

"Lucien," she repeated. Her fingers tightened their grip on his arm. "None of that was your fault."

"I know that consciously," he said. "It takes two people to fall in love, and while we had a difficult patch, we still cared about each other. *She* still loved me. And I lived, and she didn't."

Calla didn't reply and instead fixed her gaze on him with a look he couldn't fully decipher. He saw pity and compassion in her eyes, but something else. Something warm and kind.

She understood his grief.

"Have you ever lost anyone?" he asked.

"Not the way you have."

He felt like an idiot. Of course, she'd lost everyone in her life, her way of life itself.

"I've never loved anyone," she confessed. "My people don't really rally around it the way humans do. We have families and offspring, but most of us don't commit to each other as you and Emmaline did."

A new crack of thunder boomed. Lucien thought he heard the windows shake in their casements. His mind wandered for a few seconds about the state of the house. Updates aside, Greaves Estate was an old building. He hoped he wouldn't have to deal with a flood or property damage, and by extension, Edwin Hammond.

"You're daydreaming," said Calla.

"It's hardly daylight out there," Lucien said sheepishly. He glanced at the ornate brass cuckoo clock hanging on the wall. The cuckoo never emerged from its little door, but the clock itself still told time. "It's only two o'clock."

She rose to her feet. "I think I'll take a swim after all."

Lucien did likewise. "Are you mad?"

"Mad about swimming, yes," she said. "I feel, I don't know, itchy if I don't shift for at least a little while every day. I've swum through worse storms than this, and the weather isn't terrible enough yet for me to do it in the bathtub. I'll say hello to you from outside the ballroom."

Lucien had already declared that today was to be his day of rest, so he didn't want to go back to writing. Inspiration struck him. "What about the boathouse?"

"What about it?"

"The boathouse has an empty slip," he said. "I can stay on the dock. I suppose housing a full-sized boat on the property was too out of the question when the estate's builder wanted a subterranean ballroom."

She stared at him like he was speaking in tongues. "What in all the hells does a boathouse have to do with a subterranean ballroom?"

"Nothing," he said. "Just… they're both related to the water. Forgive me."

Talking about Emmaline had scrambled something in his brain. It felt like he'd just used a muscle for the first time after an injury, a good kind of pain.

"All right," said Calla. "I've never had a cup of tea on the dock while I was in mermaid form."

"I beg your pardon?"

"Tea," she repeated. "You're bringing tea to the boathouse, are you not? Since we're friends and having a nice chat while I'm in my other form?"

It was pouring rain outside during a chilly October in the north.

He was going to enjoy tea with a mermaid while she splashed around an empty slip.

"Of course," Lucien replied. "Where were my manners when I forgot to mention it?"

CHAPTER 10

*L*ucien sat on the dock, back to the wall, nursing a cup of tea while Calla swam. Occasionally, she would duck under the water and leave Lucien's company to exercise beneath the stormy sea for a few moments, but she preferred it this way: arms holding her up on the dock while her lower half gently treaded water, chatting with Lucien.

There was a lightness about him that hadn't existed a few hours ago. Calla could have sworn some of the tension lines that bracketed his eyes and mouth had disappeared like a major burden was finally lifted off his shoulders.

But that was exactly what happened, wasn't it? He'd never told anyone else about his late wife and their last years of marriage, never shared that burden with anyone. In a strange way, she felt honored to be trusted with that information.

She was looking at the face of a man who had forgiven himself when he'd done nothing wrong.

Lucien refilled her teacup from the pot he brought outside with him. "I like this," she said, looking around the boathouse. The small boat Lucien capsized from was hanging on the wall from a hook, beside a couple of other similar boats.

"The boathouse or the company?"

"Both," she said.

She meant it and hoped he understood that. She had grown to care for him in a way she never had for anyone else.

The wind picked up outside, raindrops splattering against the stupid, useless window cut into the boathouse's roof. The temperature had dropped considerably, although Calla didn't feel it much. But Lucien was wrapped up in his coat, gloved hands clutching his teacup for warmth. She didn't know how much time had passed since they left the study and its map, but it was long enough for Lucien's cheeks to grow pink with the chill.

She could spend hours swimming in the sea around the estate, and she had the feeling Lucien would stay out here, too, even if she ordered him inside. The absolute last thing she wanted to have happened was him catching a cold.

Or influenza. Calla thought of Emmaline, and a ripple of fear, mixed with sadness for Lucien, threaded through her. She had never been especially close with anyone in her life—mermaid society didn't work that way—but she was with him, and she couldn't bear the thought of losing him the same way he lost Emmaline.

"I think it's time to go inside," said Calla.

She thought relief might have crossed Lucien's face at the mention of the warm house, but he quickly replaced it with a smile. "Perfect timing," he said. "The teapot's empty."

Calla drained the rest of her cup in a couple of gulps, then braced against the dock to haul herself out of the water. "Do you want some help?" Lucien asked. "I won't fall in this time."

She was perfectly capable of getting out without help, but she still nodded. "Yes, please."

He got up and held out his hands. Calla eyed his gloves dubiously. "Aren't you worried about getting them wet?"

"I wouldn't have offered if I did," he said, but he stripped them off and stuck them in his pocket, anyway.

She shrugged and held on to them.

He pulled her out with more grace than she expected but didn't set her down right away. "Um," said Calla, looking down.

She couldn't stand up on her tail, and it would take a moment for her to shift. As it was, she held on to Lucien's shoulders for dear life, and once he realized what he'd done, his hands instinctively reached down to her lower half to keep her from falling back into the water and taking him with her. He picked her up and cradled her against him before that could happen.

His bare fingers touched her scales, and she stiffened.

It was an automatic reaction to a strange and unaccustomed feeling. No human had ever touched her scales while she was in her mermaid form. She was surprised at how good it felt.

Just as quickly, worry sank in. What if he was repulsed by her and her physiology, so very different from his?

Her fears were allayed when she saw the look on his face. There was a tenderness there that she hadn't expected, unbothered by the feel of her body in its mermaid form against his skin or the cold water that had to be seeping through his clothes.

Oh, gods, I forgot about the water.

Fish and mermaids alike tended to forget when they were wet.

"What do you think?" Calla asked.

"About what?" There was an odd huskiness to his voice she hadn't heard before.

She flipped her tail a little. "This."

"It's a part of who you are, and I like you. Ergo, I like your scales and fins."

Words she never thought she would hear, didn't know she needed to hear them, warmed her in a way tea or a furnace or a hot meal never could.

"Although I think this backfired a bit," Lucien said. "I was only going to help you out of the water, but I think I helped too much."

She had the oddest urge to lean her head against his shoulder and stay that way for a while, but the weather and her own sodden form would prove to be uncomfortable for him sooner rather than later. "I still like it," Calla said. "No one's picked me up before."

Lucien was bending to set her down on the wooden dock and let her shift more easily, and she already missed the feel of being in his arms. He gave another curious look at her tail. But before she started her shifting process, she twitched her fins experimentally again. "You can touch it if you like."

The offer had taken Lucien by surprise. "I beg your pardon?"

"My tail," she explained patiently. "How many times have you had the chance to see a real, live mermaid?" A teasing note slipped into her voice. "We aren't real to humans, remember."

Lucien crouched closer to where her fins were and experimentally touched her fins. An unexpected bolt of pleasure raced through her, every nerve in her body alert. She gasped, drawing a look from Lucien.

What in the hells?

That had never happened with anyone else, but then again, only other merfolk had touched her while she was in mermaid form.

"Do I feel like a fish?" she couldn't help but ask.

He raised an eyebrow at her question. "Not at all. You're far warmer, and your scales feel strong." Color touched his cheeks. "Your tail is beautiful."

She basked in his compliment the way she would sun herself on a rock if such an activity were safe. The way he was looking at her made her forget about the scars lining her body and her chopped-down gills and made her feel like the beautiful, mythical creature humans believed mermaids to be.

His fingers trailed past her fins, to her tail proper, gliding along her coppery-green scales, and a shudder of pleasure ran through her. She closed her eyes for a second, savoring the feeling.

When she opened them, the first thing she saw was Lucien's expression and the question in his eyes that barely masked the lust she saw reflected there. "Can I...?" he asked, voice trailing off.

She gave him the barest of nods. "I want you to."

His hands lightly traced her scales as they slid up her body until they reached her midsection, where her scales met her more human-like skin. His touch was gentle and feather-light but electric all the same.

His hands stilled just below her ribcage. Her chest rose and fell with labored breaths she hadn't known she was making until he stopped, his eyes flickering to her exposed breasts. Her nipples peaked under the intensity of his gaze.

Lucien had seen her naked plenty of times, and not once had she caught a lascivious glance from him. Her mind quickly flashed back to their first meeting when she rescued him from the sea and dragged him back into the house. He came to consciousness with her wearing a table-cloth to protect both of their modesties, to add a layer of normalcy to what had to be the most bizarre experience of his life up to that point.

But he'd never leered at her, and he wasn't now. For the first time since her exile and torture, Calla felt beautiful under someone else's gaze.

But his hands didn't move. Nor did the rest of him, poised over her like a man about to kiss his lover.

Neither of them moved for a moment, not wanting to spoil what could happen.

It was the lack of water immersion that ruined it for Calla. Her body insisted on shifting to human form, something that had only started recently when she moved in with Lucien. She didn't know if the newly discovered urge occurred due to her spending so much time on dry land or a result of Isadore's experiments, but it couldn't be ignored.

She hated to do this. "Lucien," she whispered. "I have to shift."

He immediately removed his hands, and she immediately missed the feel of them on her. She resisted the impulse to apologize for something she couldn't help, and Lucien stepped away from her and turned around to give her privacy. He busied himself collecting the teapot and cups, settling them on a tray.

Shifting wasn't as painful as it used to be, but it was still uncomfortable, the pressure and strain on her lower body still having the power to induce tears to her eyes. Mercifully, it was over quickly, and she hefted herself to her feet, noting that she wasn't as shaky as she used to be.

She quickly dressed, not caring that her clothes would get wet. She pulled her dress over her head, the pink and white striped fabric still damp from her mad dash to the boathouse, and a near-sodden shawl over top. She jammed her bare feet into her boots and quickly crossed the length of the dock to join him closer to the door. "I'm ready," she said.

The rain hadn't let up at all during their time in the boathouse, and the sky was nearly dark despite it being mid-afternoon. They hurried to the servants' entrance without speaking.

Once inside, Calla stripped off her shawl and Lucien his coat, and he draped his over a chair in front of the stove to dry off. He held out his hand wordlessly, and Calla handed him her shawl.

Tension filled the air, and Calla didn't know how to make it dissipate, make it return to normal between them.

His hands on her body had changed something fundamental to her feelings for him. Although, if she was honest with herself, those feelings had been simmering since shortly after they met, and she could admit to herself how she felt now. She wanted his hands on her again, no matter what form she had taken, his lips against her skin.

She wanted to run her hands through his hair, graze her fingertips along his stubbled cheeks. See what he looked like under his carefully pressed trousers and shirt, how his skin would feel against hers.

A couple of times, Lucien looked like he wanted to say something, but then he seemed to talk himself out of it. Calla didn't press him.

The horrible notion that he wasn't attracted to her crashed through her like a tidal wave, fast and brutal. True, he'd been fascinated with her scales and tail. But one could be simultaneously interested and disgusted with something.

But the brazen lust she'd seen reflected in his expression... she was sure she hadn't imagined it.

An equally awful idea surfaced: he was attracted to her and didn't want to be.

She wasn't sure she could think about that and not cry in front of him.

I survived exile and torture, and I'm about to cry over a man.

She felt ridiculous.

And sort of grimy. Her dress was now soaked from the rain and the seawater that dripped from her hair, and she longed for the escape a warm bath would bring.

When Lucien still didn't say anything, instead turning away to the sink, where he set about cleaning the bits of tea leaves from the pot and cups, she finally broke their damnable silence. "I'm going to take a bath."

He glanced at her over his shoulder, his face unreadable and overturned silver teapot in hand, and nodded.

∼

FUCK.

Calla's favorite epithet couldn't stop itself from repeating in Lucien's mind as he cleaned the tea set they'd used in the boathouse. He returned the teapot to its fussy little stand in the dining room's old-fashioned sideboard and paced the room, occasionally walking around the table as he tried to sort out how best to repair the damage he'd done to his friendship with Calla.

He hadn't viewed her with a strictly platonic lens for some time. It wasn't seeing her nude in her mermaid form that drew his attention; it was everything else. Her strength. Her delight in activities like bowling and swimming, her curiosity about the world out of the water. Even the outlandish way she dressed, which caught his attention far more than her mermaid form did. There was something undeniably erotic about a woman whose dress buttons weren't fastened all the way and didn't wear a corset, whose long hair was left loose.

The memory of her lying on the dock in the boathouse, hair spread over her shoulders and breasts, would stay with him a long time, more memorable than her darting through the water surrounding the ballroom. But guilt stabbed at him, too.

He'd tried to play the gentleman, help her out of the water, and that backfired spectacularly.

She'd offered to let him touch her tail, her scales. He didn't know if she'd done so because she thought she *had* to.

Her scales were surprisingly warm to the touch, and her tail trembled under his hand. When their eyes met, hers were huge, pupils dilated in the same way his must have been, her chest rising and falling in short, excited breaths.

He wanted her. And he wasn't sure if he could will that impulse away.

He paused his pacing. "And it isn't because of Emmaline," he murmured. Perhaps if he talked to himself, he might receive an answer.

With none forthcoming after a few seconds, he resumed his pacing.

He made his way out of the dining room to the study, where the same bottle of whiskey he had a dram from the night he met Calla was. He rolled his eyes at the insect collection as he poured a short drink and tossed it back in a single, fiery gulp. They no longer bothered him. Replacing the bottle, he left the study and headed for the stairs.

When he reached the bathroom, he could hear splashing through the door, so he left Calla be. An image of her as a mermaid in the tub filled his mind: wet skin sparkling in the bathroom's yellow electric lights, scales shimmering. Her dark hair shining, spread over her upper body and clinging to her.

A wave of lust crashed through him, and he leaned against the wall, waiting for it to pass just enough so he didn't make an utter arse of himself.

After what felt like an interminable amount of time, he heard movement in the bathroom that meant Calla had shifted back to her human form and was drying off and dressing.

Both of her dresses need to be laundered.

Damn it all. Why did he only buy two of them for her when there were seven days in a week? The dry goods shop at the inn had to have had one more dress that wasn't mourning.

His train of thought was cut off when the door opened. Calla jumped when she saw him, and she blushed.

She wore a nightgown, the fabric so sheer he could see the tips of her breasts. Her damp hair had been combed and lay in drying curls around her shoulders.

She was the most beautiful woman he'd ever seen.

"Lucien," she breathed. Her nostrils flared like she just smelled something delicious, and her pupils dilated again as they did in the boathouse.

He stood a foot and a half from the doorway, and he dared not move. His body was tense, an urge to eliminate the distance between them and kiss her nearly over-whelming.

She moved first, taking the delicate, deliberate steps she made when she was newly shifted. She surprised him when she reached a hand to his jaw and lightly ran her fingertips over the beard growth there. It was a small touch, but it only whetted his appetite for more.

His arms looped around her waist, and he kissed her.

CHAPTER 11

*C*alla was so taken by surprise that it took a couple of seconds for her brain to register what was happening.

Lucien's lips were pressed against hers, his hands hot on her body through her underdress. Once she had recovered her bearings and realized that she wasn't hallucinating, she slid her arms around his shoulders, bringing him closer to her. She kissed him back, putting everything she felt into it.

As abruptly as he started it, Lucien stepped away.

Had she done something wrong? Hurt and confusion warred in her as she tried to read his face.

"I'm sorry," he said simply.

"What for?"

He considered the question for a few seconds before answering, "I don't know."

Calla thought she knew. "Is it guilt for something you don't need to be guilty for?"

He ran his hands through his sandy hair, and she guessed that she was correct. He looked like he was trying

137

to decide between bolting and kissing her again, and Calla wasn't willing to let this conversation fade away unspoken.

"Kiss me, Lucien."

His blue eyes caught hers, and she could see he wanted to.

She took a tiny step forward, so her feet touched his. She could see the tension he held in his body under his clothes, how he was fighting with himself over something, instinct versus a duty he wasn't obligated to have.

Calla was about to kiss him herself when he did it again.

She was ready for him this time. Her tongue touched his lips, demanding entrance, and he willingly gave it. A moan escaped him, the noise's vibrations radiating through her body. She staggered back from the intensity of having him so close, nearly backing them into the bathroom.

Lucien righted her in time. He gently nipped at her lower lip, drawing a shudder of pleasure from her before doing the same thing with her earlobe. "Tell me no," he whispered.

She stiffened. "Why would I do that?"

"You can tell me no, and I'll listen."

"I know you would," she replied. She backed her face away from his just enough to look at him. "And you need to know that I want this. I wanted it before, too." She leaned her forehead against his. "You're looking at me like I'm a dessert, and you haven't had a dessert in weeks."

He laughed. It was an unexpected and very welcome thing to hear, and the anxiety she'd been holding on to about him unwound itself. But his mirth evaporated as soon as it appeared, replaced with something more solemn. "I don't want you to think you're obligated," he said.

"Obligated to do what?"

She was being deliberately obtuse, she knew. But she

wanted no secrets or reservations about physical contact between them. She respected him too much.

"Anything," he replied. "I want you, more than you could know. But I can wait or abstain altogether." He threaded his fingers through hers, holding their hands between them. "I only want this if you do."

She traced the backs of his fingers with her thumbs, how his skin managed to feel soft and roughened at the same time. "I do," she said quietly.

This time, she kissed him first, her arms winding around his neck to touch his hair like she wanted to. He moved his hands back to where her hips met her backside, kneading the flesh there through her underdress and pulling her closer to him. With the motion, the proof of his desire pressed against her belly.

Excitement, hot and urgent, coiled inside her like a spring at the ready.

He broke their contact, sweeping her up in a hold the way he did when she was in her mermaid form in the boathouse. She gave a startled shriek, then leaned into him and nuzzled her lips against his neck, lightly scoring him with her teeth. He sucked in a harsh breath, then, with her cradled against him, carried her through the corridor.

She could guess where he was headed; the only question was if it was his bedroom or hers.

He stopped in front of his and nudged the door open with his foot. "I wanted to do that in the boathouse," he confessed.

"Carry me naked across the threshold?"

His eyes darkened. "Why not?"

He set her down, and he raised a hand to rest it on her underdress's shoulder strap. She stepped away a few inches. "Wait."

Lucien immediately stilled.

"You've seen me naked plenty of times," she said. Her heart pounded in anticipation to rival the thunder booming outside. "I want my turn."

But before either of them could do anything, she glanced around the room for a light source. A hurricane oil lamp rested on the dressing table, and she turned up its flame, lighting up the room in the stormy darkness.

Lucien's fingers were already working on the bottom button of his vest. He slid it off his shoulders and tossed it away, unconcerned with where it landed. As he started working on his shirt buttons, he said, "You don't have to be in the altogether to be alluring."

The compliment warmed her in a way his kisses and caresses hadn't. A tiny part of her worried that he would take greater notice of her scars and ruined gills if she left a lamp on, but she should've known he wouldn't care.

Lucien continued. "I'm not sure you understand what you look like in a dress without undergarments, for example." His shirt was halfway unbuttoned now, and he pulled it free from his waistband to unfasten the rest of them. When he looked at her, she saw his eyes were half-hooded with desire. "It's distracting. And my favorite part of that is you don't care if anyone else likes it."

"But you do," Calla said, more to herself.

"You have no idea." Shirt unbuttoned, he didn't move to take it off. Instead, he closed the distance between them and untied one of her underdress shoulder straps. The rasp of his calloused fingertips sent sparks dancing along her skin, lighting up her entire body as readily as she lit the oil lamp.

He tilted up her face with the same hand to give himself enough space to dust featherlight kisses along her throat and collarbone. When his lips found the spot under her ears where her gills had been severed, she stiffened involuntarily.

He stilled, too, following her lead. "Too much?" he whispered in her ear. "Should I stop?"

An unwelcome wave of shame flowed through her when she thought of her mutilated gills. "No," she said. "It's just—my gills. What's still there, anyway. They're ugly."

She didn't want to say it, lest he believe her, but he'd asked.

"No, they aren't," he said. "No one who knows you or looks at you would ever think that."

His reassurances offered a great deal of relief to Calla. "Then prove it," she said, daring him. "Show me."

That was all the encouragement he needed. His tongue traced a line along her gills to her ear before biting the lobe with just enough possessive force to wrench a sharp gasp from her. Her hands reached under his open shirt to run along the planes of his chest to his abdomen, causing his breath to quicken. As she toyed with the buttons on his trousers, one of his hands came between them to pull down her underdress just enough to expose her breast.

Calla forgot about his trousers as his fingers found her nipple, plucking it until it formed a hard peak. She didn't object when he reached for the other strap, finally pushing the garment down around her waist.

And then she remembered who was supposed to be getting naked.

"This was supposed to be your turn," she said.

He shrugged off his shirt, revealing broad shoulders that Calla couldn't help but reach out and touch. "I'm enjoying finally touching you," he said, giving her a knowing smile.

Still, he unbuttoned his trousers and made short work

of them, tossing them and his undergarments and socks away.

Calla finally had her wish.

His broad shoulders and chest gave way to a narrow waist and hips. His thighs looked as powerful as she thought they must be when he picked her up and carried her, and their muscles flexed as he strode toward her, hands pushing her underdress down so she could step out of it. His erection bobbed against her hip, and she reached between their bodies to slide her hand around it.

He closed his eyes and hissed. "If you keep that up, this is going to be over before it starts."

Calla let him go with some reluctance.

He took her face in his hands and kissed her, tongue demanding entrance to her mouth, which she was only too happy to give. Her nipples scraped against his hard chest, and she had to pull away for a few seconds to catch her breath. Her legs felt like they would give out from under her.

Lucien noticed that immediately and gave a pointed look at the bed.

She bit her lip and nodded.

His mouth slanted over hers, and he guided her to the bed until her knees hit the back of the mattress. She leaned back, taking him with her, and gripped the bedcovers to pull herself closer to the center of the mattress. Lucien followed her lead, skin to skin against her, alternating between kissing and lightly nipping her neck. This time, when his lips touched her scarred gills, she wasn't self-conscious about it. He made her feel like someone to be cherished.

His mouth moved lower, across her collarbone to her breast, taking in one nipple and then the other. Her hips instinctively lifted toward him in a pale imitation of what she really wanted, and his hand rested against it, running the calloused pad of his thumb against her skin. It was such a small gesture, but it still made her shiver.

There was a knowing look on his face when he raised his head to look at her, and his hand slid lower, between her legs, where he found her wet and ready. He slipped a finger into her, and at hearing Calla's gasp, said, "More?"

She nodded. She didn't want him to ever stop.

He pushed a second finger into her, moving them in a tempo that already had her wanting more as soon as he started. She locked her hands around his neck and pulled her to him, mouths meeting in a clash of lips and tongues, a silent plea from her to replace his fingers with something else.

Lucien laced her fingers through his and placed her hands on either side of her head as he angled his body over hers. He lined himself up at her entrance, and in one smooth motion, pushed forward.

He stilled for a few seconds inside her, catching his breath, and Calla did likewise. She hooked a leg around his hips, urging him deeper. He groaned, muffing the sound against her neck as he worked his way into her body.

Ecstasy crashed through her, drawing a full-throated cry from somewhere deep in her body as he carved a place in her, marking her as his. She pulled her hand out from where he'd pinned it to grab his hair and kiss him, his harsh breath against her a sign that he was nearing his climax, too.

His name was on her lips as he came, then wordlessly rolled over, taking her with him. Lucien's arm wrapped around her, and she snuggled against his chest, listening to his still rapidly beating heart.

Rain pounded itself against the windows, and she thought there could be no better place to be.

～

CALLA'S BREATH had grown deeper and more even, but Lucien knew she hadn't dozed off. A couple of times, she traced lines on his chest with her fingertip, as if studying and memorizing his body to reflect on it later.

He pulled the bedcovers closer around them. "Are you cold?" she asked.

"Your body temperature is warmer than anyone else I've ever known," Lucien said. "But yes, the part of me you aren't draped over is chilled."

Her laugh rumbled through him, and Lucien tightened his hold on her in response.

It felt incredibly natural, so right, to be in here with her in bed right now. If he could stay in this moment forever, he would. No responsibilities to take care of, no books to write, no editors to keep in touch with.

But the reality was at some point soon, he would have to turn in his new book and return to London and continue rebuilding his life there. Calla would take that dirigible journey to Scotland. Now that they could name the places she couldn't return to—the Irish Sea and the coast off of Liverpool—it would be easier to pick a new spot on the map for her to resettle.

And both of them would be alone again.

His earlier suggestion that she come back to London with him resurfaced in his mind. She said she would think about it, and the subject hadn't been brought up again. Was now a good time to mention it?

What the devil, why not? "Calla, do you remember when I asked if you would consider moving to London?"

Her finger stilled over his heart. He hoped that wasn't a harbinger of things to come. "Yes."

"You said you would think about it." Shyness overcame

him, absolutely ridiculous considering what they had just shared. "Have you?"

She relaxed again and draped her arm over his chest in a possessive embrace he liked. "Are you asking me that out of obligation?"

"What kind of obligation?"

She raised her head to look at him, incredulity in her eyes. "We just spent the afternoon fu—"

"No," Lucien said quickly. "I want you to come back with me because I like you. I care about you, that's all. I can help you navigate this world while you figure it out."

"Navigate," she said and snickered.

"What's so amusing about the word 'navigate'? It doesn't have any sexual connotations I'm unaware of, does it?"

"I'm a mermaid," she said as if that should be obvious. "You know, mermaids and the water. We're born with the ability, and humans learn navigation skills. Routes are navigated when mermaids and people are in it." She let out a dramatic sigh. "The best jokes are the ones that have to be explained."

"I didn't make a joke."

"I was trying to—never mind," she said. Lucien was already smiling at her frustration. But it left his face with her next words. "My navigation skills aren't quite what they used to be."

And that was all thanks to Isadore's experiments, which brought the conversation back around to the danger Calla was still in. They had guessed the city Isadore was likely in, but Lucien had no idea as to how to locate him down personally. Nor did he have any acquaintances who would know how to look for a madman performing experiments on mermaids.

A horrible thought seized Lucien, deeply unwelcome, as he idly stroked Calla's hair.

What if Isadore had captured another mermaid?

"Lucien?" Calla lifted her head again and turned on her side to more easily face him. "What's wrong?"

There was no point in lying to her. Not that he wanted to, but he still couldn't help but ask, "How can you tell?"

"You breathe differently when you're upset about something," she said. She levered herself up on one arm to support her head. "Tell me."

He hated to ruin the moment they were having and hesitated, trying to form the words that would do just that.

Calla poked him in the chest. "*Lucien.*"

"What if Isadore kidnapped another mermaid?" he asked. "One of your people, or a mermaid from another... pod, I suppose." It occurred to him that he didn't know what a group of mermaids called themselves.

But the news didn't shock Calla as badly as he thought it would. "It's possible," she said slowly. "But unlikely."

"How can that be?"

"Because no other mermaid in our clan is as stupid as I was when it came to interacting with humans," she said. "I took a lot more risks than the others. I told you some of my people would shift and take a human lover, but it wasn't commonplace. No one lingered around harbors like I did, especially after I was exiled. I was much more careless after that happened." She bit her lip, a gesture he recognized she did when she was feeling self-conscious. "I don't think I cared as much if I lived or died until Isadore caught me in a net. I didn't know how much I wanted to live until I was trapped in that tank." She sniffled. "He has a submersible for deep-sea exploration. That's how he got me. I wasn't paying attention, and the next thing I knew, I was covered in a net and couldn't get out."

"None of that was your fault," Lucien said gently. He turned on his side as well, mirroring her movement. "You did nothing to bring this on yourself. You were all alone, and someone took advantage of that."

Calla's eyes were suspiciously shiny when he said those words, but she didn't cry or contradict him. "Thank you."

"What for?"

"A lot of things," she said. "Not being afraid when I told you what I am. For trying to teach me to read even though I complain about it."

"You can spell out our names and sound out words," Lucien said. "You've picked up quite a lot in a short period of time."

She blushed a little under his praise. "You helped me figure out where Isadore came from and showed me how big the world is."

"I haven't shown you any of that other than the globe."

"Would you stop telling me the ways you think you haven't helped me?" There was a smile on her face as she made the request, so Lucien knew she wasn't too serious. "You taught me how to bowl. Does London have bowling lanes?"

A tiny spark of hope flared in him at the question. "Yes. And I'm not sure I taught you how to bowl since I'm unfamiliar with most of the rules besides knocking down the pins."

"My point is you've been the greatest friend I've ever had," she said. "Maybe the only true one."

Now it was Lucien's turn to feel a little misty-eyed.

But that feeling was dashed when she ran her hand down his chest, his abdomen, to his cock, which immediately responded to her touch. "This, too."

She urged him on his back, something Lucien was only too happy to comply with.

"Am I to believe you like me for my body?" he asked.

She straddled him, all glorious curves visible above him. "But of course, Mr. Quinn," she said. Her nimble fingers slid along his length, and she leaned down to kiss him.

Lucien whimpered. "It isn't nice to tease."

"But it's fun."

And he'd asked her not to during their earlier coupling. He could lie back and enjoy it now, now that she had found her pleasure, too.

"And I like you for you," Calla said, uncharacteristically serious for a few seconds. She angled her body over his. "This is a benefit I'm pleased to have discovered."

As she worked him into her body and set his nerves aflame all over again, a tiny, rational part of him remembered that she still hadn't agreed to accompany him back to London.

CHAPTER 12

*C*alla woke up alone in Lucien's bed the following morning, the cloudless sky a crisp blue visible through the half-open drapes. She stretched, noting a few places on her body where her muscles protested, and got out of bed.

She padded around the bedroom until she found Lucien's dressing gown. She slid into the too-large garment and tied it around her waist before making her way through the estate in search of him.

Lucien was in the subterranean ballroom, wearing wrinkled trousers and a shirt left untucked and mostly unbuttoned. He was barefoot, too, a rarity. She smiled. Maybe she was rubbing off on him.

Speaking of rubbing… there were a couple of spots on her neck where his beard stubble grazed her skin a little too harshly.

He looked up when he heard her limp down the stairs, although her walking abilities had greatly increased in the preceding days. "Good morning," he said. He set down his pen and set aside the music stand he used as a makeshift desk. He stood up and reached for her as soon as she descended the last step on the spiral staircase, pressing a kiss to her lips that took her breath away. "You looked so peaceful I didn't want to wake you up. I've been awake for hours."

"Your book?"

He smiled. "It's complete."

Calla dashed to the music stand where his folder rested, a few handwritten pages atop it. "It is?"

"I wrote 'The End' about half an hour ago," he said. "I've just been making some notes to send to my editor. I'll walk into town later to send a telegram to him just so he knows."

"You'll have to read it to me someday," Calla said.

"Of course. Just because I've been complaining about it doesn't mean I don't want people to enjoy my stories." He tucked a lock of hair behind her ear and let his finger-tips trail along her skin. She could've sworn she felt sparks as she did that, and she shivered. "And soon, you'll be able to read them for yourself."

"Maybe so, but I'd still like to listen to you read them," said Calla. "Picture the two of us, my head in your lap…"

"Very little reading would get done if you did that."

"I could test your will while you read to me. I'm sure I can think of a few ways."

"You test it all the time," Lucien said. "And I would love nothing more than to discover your different methods. But until then, I have to feed you and then walk to the post office and send that telegram."

"You don't have to feed me," she objected. "I can feed myself."

"Allow me to amend that," Lucien said. "It's nearly noon, and I could eat a meal. I'm sure you could, too."

Calla was hungry now that she mentioned it. "Can I walk into town with you, too?"

Lucien looped his arm around her waist and pulled her against him before starting the trek back upstairs. "Why not? It's a beautiful day."

～

SEEING Calla dressed as she was right now was a bit surreal to Lucien. She scowled at her reflection in the looking glass but didn't complain.

Both of them had given up on arranging her long hair in any of the current styles, and Lucien finally clumsily braided it for her. He laced her into her corset as well, not wanting to give any of Gull's End's inhabitants reason to gossip about an uncorseted lady wandering their village square, and asked her if she was certain she wanted to accompany him this afternoon.

Her coat was a little too large, and she occasionally stumbled over the dirt road leading to the village in her boots, but she still didn't voice any of her aggravation. Lucien was happy to hold on to her hand, her arm—any excuse to touch her. Once in a while, they stopped, either for Calla to take a break or to look at a plant she found interesting.

And he loved every minute of it. He hadn't known how much he would enjoy showing someone he cared about all the nice things in the world, scant as they could be.

It was the middle of the afternoon when they arrived in Gull's End, and it was as bustling as a tiny northern English village could be at this time of day. A horse was tethered to a post beside the inn, and a steam cab was left on the road in front of it. "That's unusual," Lucien said, discreetly pointing to the cab. "I wonder where it's from."

"What is it?"

"It's a steam-powered vehicle. They're much more common in the cities," he explained.

"I've never seen one before."

"I don't imagine they're common at the Liverpool docks," he said, steering her in the direction of the village post office. "And the roads here aren't designed for them. They're fussy things. They do well on paved roads." He couldn't help but look at the cab once more. "It isn't marked, either." An errant strand of hair drifted around Calla's face in the autumn breeze, and he tucked it behind her ear.

"Have you ever ridden in one?"

"They're common in London, so yes. They're more comfortable in the colder months than a hack."

Arm-in-arm, he took her to Gull's End's tiny post office. Like everyone else in the village, the proprietor was standoffish, but he was efficient and didn't pepper Lucien with irritating questions. The post office also served as the village's bookshop, with a few months-old tomes on offer.

Calla discreetly pointed to one of the bookshelves. "Are any of them yours?" she whispered.

He shook his head. "No. This isn't the type of village where the reading of adventure novels is considered an acceptable pastime." An idea struck him, one that was patently obvious. "I will have to write a book based on this village someday."

He filled out a telegram card, writing only the words BOOK COMPLETE WILL SEND SOON while Calla watched him, fascinated. He gave the card to the poker-faced postmaster and some coins to pay for it and waited.

"How does that work?" Calla asked as soon as the post-master turned his back and carried the card to the telegraph.

Her breath in his ear was a distraction that he forced himself to ignore. "I'll explain later," he promised. "For now, just pretend you've seen a telegraph before."

"I'll pretend I've seen *everything* before," she said and left his side to look at the post office's offerings. Not that there was much to look at.

Lucien watched her out of the corner of his eye while he waited for the postmaster to send his telegram. She picked up a book at random and opened it, running her hands down the pages as if the words could reveal themselves to her that way.

"Don't touch anything if you're not buying it," said the postmaster without turning around.

Calla immediately put it back. Lucien sent a sympathetic look her way.

Christ, was there *anyone* in this godforsaken village who was capable of basic manners? No wonder a property as grand as Greaves Estate had the vacancy rates it did. Lucien wondered what kind of shenanigans Gull's End inhabitants got up to that justified their treatment of visitors in such a way. He would have to make a list of possible reasons the townspeople could have to be so deranged.

Calla occupied herself looking at the newspapers, all broadsheets from major cities. "They just came in this morning," said the postmaster. "Direct."

That could explain the steam cab they saw outside the inn. Despite the warnings from his carriage driver on the way here from the Manchester airfield about the treacherous roads, evidently some people were too impatient to wait for a horse-drawn vehicle's deliveries.

When Lucien joined Calla at the rack holding stacks of fresh broadsheets, he saw her silently sounding out a word. "That says 'Liverpool,' doesn't it?" she whispered. "I recognized the L, I, V, and E."

It was an edition of the *Liverpool Intelligencer*. Lucien picked it up to check its date.

"You touched it!" snapped the postmaster.

Lucien rolled his eyes and tucked the newspaper under his arm. Turning around, he walked back to the counter and left another coin there to pay for it.

He guided Calla out of the post office. "Is everyone here so rude?" she asked, echoing his thoughts.

"I think so, yes," he replied. He looked at the inn and saw a man feeding coal into the back of the steam cab. Calla stopped to watch, and he waited with her.

Once the coal was loaded into it, the man slammed shut the fuel compartment and fired up the vehicle's oven. A belch of black smoke issued from the cab's back vent, and the man briskly walked to the vehicle's front. He let himself into the driver's seat and set the cab in motion, steering it to the dirt road. It slowly trundled along the ruts, smoke and steam billowing around it.

"Ugh," said Lucien. "The smell in that one has to be abominable. I've never seen one emit that much smoke."

Calla stared at it, intrigued, until it disappeared down the road.

Lucien took her elbow and guided her back to the road in the direction of home.

He smiled to himself. *Home.* It seemed unbelievable that a huge, weird house in the middle of nowhere had taken the place of his London flat to feel where it was where he belonged.

He slanted a glance at Calla, who was watching the road beneath them, careful to avoid stepping on excessively uneven ruts, and felt a rush of warmth at the sight. It wasn't the house that made it feel like home.

Lucien had resigned himself to being alone for the rest of his life, convinced he had nothing to offer anyone. It wasn't guilt at the prospect of betraying Emmaline, although he knew moving on at some point wasn't disrespectful to her memory. He just hadn't seen the point in seeking out happiness.

And he hadn't really sought it out now; it just happened. He'd come to Gull's End to revive his career, and he was sure Peter Fenton would like his new book. He hadn't expected to find love while he was here.

He stopped so suddenly both of them nearly tripped. "Lucien!" Calla yelped as she lurched forward.

He grabbed her around the waist to keep her upright. "Are you all right?"

"Yes, but what was that? Did you see something?"

"No," he said quickly. "Just lost in thought."

"About your new book?" They set off again.

"Yes," he lied.

He didn't know how Calla would react to hearing a declaration of love from him. As much as he wanted her to stay with him, he wouldn't stand in the way of her leaving for somewhere she felt safer. He didn't want her to feel obligated to stay with him and put her wishes on the shelf on his behalf.

He wanted her to be happy, regardless of how she chose to move forward.

WITH LUCIEN HAVING RETURNED to his underwater study to write, Calla decided to bowl instead.

Her feet and legs ached after taking her longest walk on dry land in her life, but it wasn't debilitating, and she was sure she could do it again. She was still glad to be rid of her boots, stockings, and most of her undergarments when she and Lucien returned and wore her blue dress with the top buttons unfastened.

Lucien had mentioned the night before how much he liked her wearing only that. She felt herself blush as she remembered those words and what happened after.

And now, he was acting a little strangely. She would have taken it personally had he not still been so affectionate during the walk and when they came back. He clearly had something on his mind, and hopefully, he would tell her about it when he was ready.

Before she made her way to the bowling room, she stopped in the kitchen for a drink and one of the chocolates Lucien brought home with her dresses. The newspaper he was goaded into buying at the post office had been left on a chair under the hooks where their coats hung, and out of curiosity, she picked it up.

The big words at the top read *Liverpool Intelligencer*, according to Lucien. Calla flipped through its pages, fascinated at the rows of tiny type and its pictures. Bowling forgotten, she carried her tea, chocolate, and the newspaper to the dining room. She unfolded the newspaper on the table and opened the drapes to let more light in, all the easier to read by.

She'd almost managed to sound out the name "Liverpool" in the post office; surely, she could read a few more things in the newspaper.

She pictured reading it aloud to an astonished Lucien. He would be proud of her, and kiss her, and…

I am never going to learn how to read if I keep thinking about having sex with him again.

She forced all thoughts of Lucien and what he looked like naked out of her mind and concentrated on what was before her.

"*Liverpool Intelligencer*," she murmured, running her

fingers over the words. There were smaller letters forming words beneath the title, written in capitals. Calla found capital letters easier to recognize than lowercase.

And forget handwriting, she thought. *I'll never be able to write as fluidly as Lucien does.* Cursive writing was a whole other language she didn't have the energy to learn right now.

She sounded out the letters until they reminded her of words she'd heard before, and she was able to discern, "'Published Weekly on Saturday.'"

She looked up, then looked back at the newspaper again. *Liverpool Intelligencer, Published Weekly on Saturday.*

"Fuck," Calla said softly. "I did it." Pride surged in her, and she ate her chocolate piece as a reward.

And it was Monday besides, but she supposed it took some time for a newspaper to make its way to Gull's End all the way from the cities.

She examined other capital-lettered phrases on the newspaper's front page, sounding out words that reported on a fire and another of a festival. She turned the pages, picking out other words and examining the pictures. There was nothing of importance that she could see, nothing about a missing mermaid or the madman who took her.

Did you really *expect to find something about Isadore in the newspaper? Could you even spell his name?*

She probably couldn't and would need Lucien's help. She wasn't sure if "Isadore" was spelled with an S or a Z. Or two of each. The English language was ridiculous that way.

Calla continued turning the pages, cringing at a hand-drawn illustration of a condemned man hanging from a noose. "'Murderer Johns hanged,'" she sounded out and shuddered. Why was there a picture? Who thought that was a good idea?

She quickly turned the page. A list caught her eye, and

with some difficulty was able to ascertain it was a recipe. Cooking was an interesting pursuit, but she couldn't make heads or tails of how the ingredients were listed, and besides that, most of the ingredients were completely unknown to her.

But maybe she could keep the newspaper and try out the recipe when she had a better handle on reading.

Where would you prepare it if your grand plan is to hide out in the northern Scottish waters?

She paused and set down the newspaper for a moment, considering that. The appeal of a lonely life in the North Sea had rapidly declined in favor of going to London with Lucien instead. She wouldn't have the access to open water that she would here or in Scotland, but she would be with him. They could figure out the water issue later.

He'd asked her to come back with him. She desperately wanted to say yes, but she didn't want to be a burden. She was a barely literate mermaid on the run from a madman, and she didn't want to bring unnecessary risk to someone she cared about. She had no doubt that Isadore, if he managed to hunt them down, wouldn't hesitate to kill Lucien if it meant keeping Calla and continuing his monstrous research.

Her skin prickled when she thought of Isadore, remembering his makeshift surgeries on her gills, the potions he injected her with, his taking her blood. He spoke of his fascination with shapeshifters, of his desire to find a way to further amphibious technology with what he learned from her.

She shook her head, trying to clear it of his memory, and turned the page. Hopefully, there would be something happier she could read about. Calla could use illustrations of baby animals to cheer herself up.

There was an illustration on the following page, but it

wasn't of a baby sheep or cow. She froze, her heart stop-ping for a few beats as she stared at the likeness.

Oh, no.

Tears gathered in her eyes, and she scraped the news-paper's thin pages back together and bolted from the dining room table, running as fast as her limping legs could carry her.

Lucien wrote a letter to his editor to be posted in the coming days, further detailing his new book and promising to bring him the manuscript as soon as he returned to London. Setting it aside, he began to outline his next novel, set in a cloistered village gone mad based on Gull's End, as he promised Calla he would.

His books largely revolved around known fears, the creeping dread everyone could feel when faced with a closed wardrobe door and anything unsavory behind it. He had never written anything about the supernatural, not wanting to find his work lumped in with the likes of charla-tans who claimed they could speak with the dead. But as he considered what kind of terrible secrets a Gull's End-like village could contain, he decided on something fantastic.

Perhaps the town was inhabited by vampires. He jotted down a few ideas to that effect.

The irregular sound of Calla's footsteps on the ball-room's spiral staircase had him setting aside his paper and pen, a smile on his face. But it quickly evaporated when he saw the terrified look on her face and the crumpled *Liver-pool Intelligencer* in her hands.

"Look at this," she commanded and spread out the newspaper across his music stand.

An illustration taking up half the page was displayed in front of him, the subject bearing a very accurate likeness of Calla.

Lucien's blood ran cold. "Do you know what this says?" he asked.

She shook her head, tears streaming down her cheeks. "I didn't take the time to try to sound it out," she said. A short, bitter laugh escaped her. "You should've seen me with the front page, though. I did so well."

"Calla," he said, taking his hands in hers. She was shaking like a leaf. So was he, but he hoped she wouldn't notice.

"What does it say?"

A lump had formed in his throat, stubborn and determined to stay no matter how much he swallowed. "That you're a missing person from Liverpool, and a reward is being offered for your return."

"Who's offering it?" she asked between sobs.

His heart felt like it was being torn in two, seeing her terror. "An Isadore Smythe."

She cried harder and threw herself into his arms. He immediately hugged her back, not wanting to ever let her go.

Knowing Isadore's surname provided a small measure of comfort to Lucien, but he didn't mention that yet. Besides, it could be a pseudonym.

"I have to leave," she sobbed into his shoulder.

"We'll both leave," he said. "We can hide out in London. You can stay in my flat."

"I can't put you in that kind of danger."

"London's a big city," Lucien protested. "Even if he thinks to look for you there, he won't find you. He's probably placed this advertisement in all the papers delivered to seaside towns and port cities, places with the easiest access to the water. Please, Calla, I can help you."

"I have to get to the North Sea," she said. "We'll both be safe with me there."

"Please consider what I'm saying," Lucien pleaded. "If you want to get to the North Sea, by God, I'll help you, but I think I can be more helpful at your side."

What he said made a lot of sense, but so did simply taking off and hiding, as her original escape plan detailed.

Matters of the heart made everything so much more complicated.

"When could we leave?" she asked.

He looked visibly relieved to hear her say "we." "I will have to hire a cab to take us to the Manchester airfield," he replied. "I will take a trip to the post office and send a telegram to the airfield to arrange that. It will be a few days before we get there. Then we'll take a dirigible to London and figure out where to go from there." His voice softened. "Will that set your mind at ease?"

"It seems too simple," she said, but she sounded more convinced than a moment ago.

"Getting away from the seaside will take you out of immediate danger," he said. He wondered how many people had seen the newspaper notice.

Certainly more than had seen her in the flesh. That number was in the single digits.

Would Edwin Hammond and Edna Claxton recognize and turn her in?

His breathing stilled. Calla noticed it immediately. "Lucien?"

Hammond and Mrs. Claxton clearly disapproved of Lucien and Calla's presence at the estate, but would they read the *Liverpool Intelligencer* and recognize the sketch?

Lucien didn't want to take that chance. "Tomorrow," he said. "Tomorrow, I'll send that telegram. And if anyone asks about you in the village, I'll say that you've moved on."

WEAK SUNLIGHT SHIVERED across the bed, rousing Lucien from sleep. He turned to his side, where Calla still rested, looking deceptively peaceful in her slumber.

He'd felt her terror at seeing her picture in the newspaper the day before, as acutely as if it was his own. He had nearly bolted back to the Gull's End post office to send another telegram, but logic told him that by the time he returned, it would likely be closed for the day. He would have to wait, anyway.

And he didn't want to be separated from Calla any more than necessary. Not when she had agreed to return to London with him.

Calla's eyes fluttered open.

"Good morning," he said. "Did you sleep well?"

"Better than I would've if I'd been alone." She snuggled against him. "What about you?"

"As best as I could under the circumstances, I suppose."

"You're going back to the post office today?"

"Yes." He pressed a kiss to the top of her head. "I'll leave after breakfast. Will you be all right here?"

She lifted her head. "I kind of want to swim while you're away, but that's how Isadore got me last time."

"There's a deep-sea diving suit in the boathouse," Lucien said, trying to lighten the mood a little.

"You don't know how to use one of those." She gave him a look that brooked no argument. "You would have told me that already if you did."

"All right then, I'll use the boat."

"Are you trying to scare me to death? You will do no such thing."

Despite the gravity of the situation, Lucien loved this early morning banter with her, wishing it could last forever.

Her fingers trailed over his chest, and she tilted her face to him. "I need you whole." She lightly bit his ear and let her hand wander down his body below the bedsheets.

"Is my body all you care about?"

She wrapped her hand around his arousal. "Oh, I like your mind, too," she purred. "Even if you haven't read any of your books to me yet."

"Are you that interested in melodramatic adventure stories with improbable plots?"

Calla straddled him, thighs balanced on either side of his hips. "Do you really think of your own work like that?" she asked without a trace of her previous flirtatiousness. "I'm sure they make people happy."

"Not as happy as I am with you."

She silenced him with a kiss, her tongue demanding entrance, which he willingly gave. "I'm being serious," she said when she broke away. "You're successful enough to earn a living with your books. You should be proud of them."

"I am," he said, voice strained.

"Then why do you sound like you aren't?"

"Because a beautiful woman is on top of me, and we're both naked? What did you expect?"

She laughed, a throaty sound he could listen to all day. He was happy to indulge her if it meant she was distracted from Isadore for a while.

Oh, hell. I would indulge her no matter what the circumstances.

He gripped her hips, angling her body over him.

"Well?" said Calla. "I'm on top of you, and we're both naked. What are you waiting for?"

Their bodies met halfway as he surged upward and she bore down. And for a while, both of them seemed to forget their troubles.

～

THE CLANG of chimes ringing through the house woke them up from a light slumber, and Lucien was the first one out of bed.

"What in the hells is that?" muttered Calla. "Are we about to die?"

Lucien slipped into his dressing gown and kissed her. "It's the doorbell."

"Why does it have to be so loud?" She threw the bedcovers over her head.

"I believe whoever is at the door is repeatedly pressing the button," Lucien called as he left the room.

"Tell whoever it is that I hate them," said Calla.

He smiled as he descended the stairs and made his way to the foyer. The caller would probably be either Hammond or Mrs. Claxton, with either of them irritated that Lucien expected privacy in his rented home.

He opened the door and found the latter waiting on the stoop, an enormous basket over her arm. Mrs. Claxton regarded Lucien with a critical eye, not bothering to hide her distaste. "Mr. Quinn," she said by way of greeting. "Do you know what time it is?"

"I haven't checked the clocks yet."

"It is half-past ten," she said. "And you are still undressed." Without waiting for an invitation, she brushed past him and headed straight for the kitchen.

"Pleasure to see you, too, Mrs. Claxton," Lucien said, following her.

While she put away groceries, Lucien prepared a pot of tea. "Fancy a cup?" he asked.

She looked at him like he'd just suggested they sacrifice a squirrel. "No, thank you."

An idea struck him, one that could shorten his time on errands today. "Mrs. Claxton, how did you get here today?"

She tilted up her chin in a weird show of defiance. "My husband drove me."

"In a steam cab?" He already knew the answer because he would have heard such a vehicle, assuming it could even be navigated on the excuse for a road. But she had gone out of her way to be rude to him and Calla. He didn't mind needling her a little.

"Certainly not. My husband and I have a cart and horse that suits us fine."

"May I offer you payment if you could drive me into the village?" he asked. "I have to go to the post office. I can make my own way back here."

Mrs. Claxton stilled in front of the icebox, a wrapped chicken in her hands. "How much?"

"One pound."

It was a stupid amount of money to pay for such a short trip, but Lucien desperately wanted to reach the post office as soon as he could.

The cook sighed. "All right. Get dressed, and be ready to go in fifteen minutes. I'm not waiting around."

CHAPTER 13

*C*alla didn't know what to do with herself while Lucien was away, so she whiled away the time in the bath. It wasn't the same as stretching out in the open water, but it provided a measure of relief to her aching muscles that begged to shift.

She had never shifted so much in her life until she met him, nor had she ever known mermaids who did. It was certainly getting easier. She no longer felt like she was being ripped apart and knitted back together every time she did so, and she could now watch the process with a strange fascination. Seeing coppery-gold scales form out of her skin, and watching the scales flatten themselves out, was engrossing. She almost understood Isadore's fascination with them.

She squeezed her eyes shut at the memory of him plucking out a scale from her midsection. She'd cried and bled bright red blood into his homemade tank.

And for what purpose was his torture?

Isadore had proclaimed an interest in shapeshifters, what he called "hybrid humans." Mermaids, werewolves.

He'd explained what a werewolf was, then claimed there was no way wolves populated Great Britain, let alone wolf-human creatures, but he'd been positive about the existence of mermaids. He had even gone so far as to commission the construction of a submersible boat to trawl the waters off the English coast to look for them, which was how he'd captured her.

He'd wanted to know where Calla's people lived, and she never told him. She was proud that she hadn't broken under his torment, but it wasn't just because she wanted to protect them. She had no idea the place where they lived was called the Irish Sea until Lucien told her. Now that she knew the name of the place, maybe she could figure out a way to get back to them and warn them.

Her sense of direction was irreparably destroyed thanks to a couple of the things Isadore injected her with. But there could be another method for her to navigate her way through the waters.

If only there was a way to alert the world's werewolves of Isadore's existence. Calla had never heard of them before Isadore kidnapped her, but they were bound to exist.

She hoped they could successfully keep to themselves, stay safe.

A knock at the bathroom door made her jump, and some water splashed from the tub. "Calla?" said Lucien from the other side. "Are you in there?"

She nodded, then remembered he couldn't see her. "Come in."

The door opened, and Lucien stuck his head inside. He sat down on the tiled floor next to the tub, an appreciative look on his face. Calla flicked a few water droplets in his direction with her tail, bringing a smile to his face. "I sent the telegram to the airfield," he said. "I should have a response by tomorrow."

"So, you'll have to walk back to the village?"

He nodded. "Or the postmaster will send the telegram along with Hammond if he gets it in his head to come here. He's due to check the property in the next day or two, anyway." He stretched out his legs and leaned back. "I'm going to tell him you moved on if he asks."

"How would I leave?" Calla countered. "If one has to send a telegram for transport, how did I get away?"

"I thought about this on the walk home," Lucien said. "If he asks, I'll tell him you left via bicycle."

"What's a bicycle?"

"It's a human-powered form of transport," Lucien replied. "I'll sketch a couple of models out for you when you get out of the bath, so you'll know what they look like. But it's a completely plausible way for a woman traveling on her own and who occasionally wears trousers to move herself through the world."

"How did I acquire this bicycle? You said you told Hammond and the village shopkeeper that I lost everything aboard a dirigible."

"You lost your *clothing*," he reminded her. "I never mentioned anything about the loss of your beloved bicycle. As far as Gull's End is concerned, you left on it yesterday afternoon when we returned from the post office."

Calla considered his story. "Do you think Hammond will believe that?" she asked.

"I don't care if he does. The important thing is that an airfield driver arrives as soon as possible, and I spirit you away to safety in London. And I don't think anyone has ever uttered those words before."

His plan made perfect sense to Calla, and yet it seemed

too easy. It was incredible and difficult to believe that she could just literally walk away from her troubles.

She had to trust him. She knew Lucien well enough to know that he had her best interests at heart.

I do trust him. It's everyone else on dry land who's suspect.

But there was one thing she'd made a note to ask of him before he came home. "Lucien," she said, feeling a little foolish.

"What is it, love?"

His use of the word "love" made her feel warm and tingly all over in a way that had nothing to do with her bathwater, but she didn't comment on it. "Are werewolves real?"

Lucien raised an eyebrow, considering her question. "Until a short time ago, I didn't know mermaids were real, so yes, it's possible. Although I doubt there are any in England or Scotland. The wolf populations in both countries were eradicated over a century ago."

"Yes, but that's just regular wolves," Calla said. "Mermaids have been able to hide our presence for hundreds of years. Surely werewolves could do the same."

"You're right," Lucien said, surprising her. "Wolves and lycanthropes are different species. There could very well be a group of werewolves keeping to themselves somewhere on this island. Although," he leaned forward on the lounge, tenting his fingertips in thought. "I'm not going to set out looking for them. If they don't bother anyone, I vote to leave them be."

She was mollified by his answer and relieved to have had her question taken seriously. "There's something else, unrelated, that I want to talk to you about," she said.

He nodded. "I'm all ears."

"I have to find a way to get back to my people and warn them," she said.

He visibly flinched when she said that but didn't try to dissuade her.

"They probably won't want to speak to me," Calla continued. "Exile is for life. But if I can find even one person from my clan, they can tell everyone else to stay away from the English ports. They have to keep their dry land explorations limited to small beaches or by all the hells!" Her tail hit the water as her frustration welled up. "Just... they could just stay in the water. Or think of better ways to disguise themselves when they want to have human company. I want to be the only mermaid this happens to." She gestured at the gills around her neck and upper body. They were healing but slower than she would have liked.

"Calla, may I ask about your parents?"

The question caught her off-guard. "Yes, I suppose. What about them?"

"Why didn't they defend you when you were cast out?"

Calla felt nothing when she thought of her parents. Not a single scrap of affection. "Mermaids aren't close to their children the way humans are," she said. "Maybe that comes from our relation to fish, I don't know. But once we're old enough to fend for ourselves, we live fairly independently. I lived near some acquaintances in a burrow of my own when I was, I don't know, twelve or thirteen." She'd interacted with her parents in the fifteen or so years since then, but those instances were casual. Unlike humans, mermaids didn't form family units. Her mother had gone on to have more children with other males, and her father did likewise with females.

"There was no point in appealing to them," she continued. "Our society doesn't work that way."

"Have other mermaids been cast out? What happened to them?"

She shrugged. "Not in my lifetime. I don't know what

other mermaids would do after banishment. I just kept on swimming, looking for somewhere new to live, until the loneliness got too much, and I got careless enough for Isadore to take me. I don't know where I would find other mermaid clans or if they would even accept an outsider."

The water had grown cold, and she didn't want to dwell on her exile any longer. She pulled the stopper from the bathtub's drain and watched the water swirl away.

This time, shifting to human form was the easiest it had been so far. She was steadier on her feet than usual and let Lucien wrap her in a towel to dry her off.

He seemed to have picked up on her need to change the subject. "Let's get a drink," he suggested. "Then I'll read to you for a while. How does that sound?"

She nodded. "Perfect."

THE FOLLOWING morning brought more gray and rainy weather, fitting for an autumn day in the north of England. But Lucien refused to let the drizzle keep him down.

He was expecting a telegram, telling him that he and Calla would be picked up at the airfield's earliest convenience.

They spent part of the morning packing his trunk, including Calla's clothes, so they could leave as soon as possible. Lucien even wrote a short note of apology to Greaves Estate's owners, apologizing for breaking his lease early. Although based on the stories Edwin Hammond told him, the surviving family members wouldn't be hurting for money. But it just felt polite. Lucien had never broken a lease before.

He and Calla spent the rest of the afternoon bowling at her request. She would miss the sport. Lucien made a mental note to see if there were any ladies' bowling leagues in London when they returned.

She's coming with me.

Every time he thought about the words, he smiled. Calla had stopped asking him about them, finally believing when he said he was happy. He could hardly believe it, either.

He still hadn't told Calla that he loved her. It felt like too much, too quickly. Based on what she told him of mermaid culture, romantic love wasn't really recognized or encouraged. He didn't know if she could or wanted to love him in return, and he couldn't bring himself to ask.

"You're doing it again," Calla said, rousing him out of his thoughts.

"Doing what?"

"Your aim is terrible, and you're smiling again."

"My aim is always terrible," Lucien said, with a glance at the end of the lane. He'd managed to knock over two pins. He half-jogged to the end and reset the pins, then picked up the ball. "And I'm smiling all the time because…" *I love you.* "I'm the happiest I've been in a long time."

Calla's expression shuttered for a few seconds, and he wondered what was wrong.

Before he could ask her, she said, "Can I ask you something personal?"

Alarm threaded through Lucien, but he forced himself to keep his voice level. "Of course, anything. We've already shared a great deal of personal information."

She bit her lip in that adorable way that meant she was overthinking something. "It's about your wife."

Perhaps she wasn't overthinking. "What about Emmaline?"

Calla didn't meet his eyes but took the ball from him.

She sent it sailing down the shiny lane without a second thought, knocking over every single pin. "I'm not her."

The alarm was replaced with confusion. "I know."

"From what you've told me, I'm the opposite of her." Something ticked in her jaw. "Is that all right?"

"What?" He could scarcely believe what he was hearing. "Yes. You're not her, and I don't expect you to try to be."

"I'm not a lady," Calla said.

"I'm not a gentleman. It was a point of contention in our marriage, as I've told you."

"I can't read."

"You're greatly improving," Lucien objected. "You've made remarkable strides in your literacy skills."

"Are you going to get bored with me?" she asked.

Before he could answer, she reset the pins and retrieved the ball, carrying it against her hip.

Lucien was astonished by the question and a little hurt. But he thought back to her description of the mermaid culture, how no one formed permanent partnerships. "No," he said, more harshly than intended. Seeing the stricken look on her face, he softened his tone. "No," he repeated. "If anything, I would be more concerned with you losing interest in me."

"Because of the other mermaids," she whispered. Understanding dawned on her face.

He nodded. "Yes."

"I'm an idiot."

"No, you aren't." He tried to hug her, but the bowling ball made that difficult. Calla shook her head a little and sent it down the lane. All but one pin collapsed. "I think that was my turn."

"I was going to win, anyway," she said.

"You were keeping score?"

"Always." Her shoulders relaxed a little. Whether it was from releasing the tension she'd been holding when she compared herself with Emmaline or from the bowling ball, Lucien couldn't say. But her expression was still serious. "I want you to want me for me," she said, her voice nearly a whisper. "And I've never done this before. I've never lived with anyone or in a city."

"I know, and I don't care." He took a deep breath, steeling himself.

I should tell her I love her.

It was stupid to delay that.

But before he could, the front door's chimes rang through the house. "Fuck!" snapped Lucien.

Calla beamed at him. "It's satisfying to hear you curse. But I think that's a bit of harsh for a visitor."

"That will probably be Hammond." He hoped the caretaker had a telegram in hand. He wanted the airfield confirmation, but damn if Hammond couldn't have had worse timing. "Go and hide, love."

"Where?"

"I'll meet you in the ballroom," he said. "You've thoroughly trounced me in bowling, and I would like to have one last studying session with you there. It's my favorite room in the house."

"Mine, too."

"I doubt I'll ever see one again," Lucien said. It would be the only thing about Gull's End that he would miss. He pressed a kiss to her lips, putting just enough promise into it that it made her gasp, and left the bowling room.

He didn't want Hammond to get impatient and let himself in before Calla had the chance to hide. Not that Lucien expected the caretaker to look in every single room, but when it came to the nosy people of Gull's End, anything was possible. Lucien could always play the role of eccentric author and refuse to let anyone into his work-space while he was still writing a novel.

The novel in question was neatly packed away in its leather holder, waiting in his trunk. But Hammond didn't know that.

The chimes rang out a second time before Lucien could open the door. A gust of cold air swept in when he did, the perfect complement to Edwin Hammond's scowl. "Good afternoon," Lucien said congenially.

Hammond removed an envelope from his coat pocket and handed it to Lucien, pinched between two gloved fingers. "Childs said you were expecting this," the care-taker said by way of greeting.

"Childs?"

"The postmaster," Hammond replied with more disdain than necessary. "You've been in twice in as many days to send telegrams."

"I'm a busy man, Mr. Hammond," said Lucien. He stepped aside to allow him access to the foyer. "I'm sure you want to come in and take a look about. Everything is as it should be."

"I'm sure you would be coming running if it wasn't." But Hammond stepped into the house and doffed his hat. "Have there been any problems since my last visit?"

Lucien shook his head. "Not one. And I should mention to you that I'll be cutting my tenancy short."

"Why?"

"My business here is finished," Lucien replied. "My book is complete, and I need to return to London and return to my life there."

"You do understand that you'll still be required to pay the rest of your rent in full?"

Lucien nodded. "The terms were plainly spelled out in the lease."

"Where is your charming cousin?" Hammond asked.

Lucien tamped down his irritation. "She's taken her leave."

"How so?" Hammond began a purposeful stride to the corridor.

Lucien followed and caught up to him. "Does that matter?"

"It's out of curiosity," Hammond replied. "She accompanied you to the post office a couple of days ago, and now she's gone without calling for a carriage to the nearest airfield."

"Calla's a bit of an odd duck," said Lucien. "She's an avid bicyclist."

Hammond halted and whirled to face Lucien. "Did she take the velocipede?" he nearly snarled.

Lucien stepped back, surprised. *Why should I be? Everyone in this village is certifiable.* "No, I didn't even know there was a velocipede on the premises." *Who the devil calls a bicycle a "velocipede" these days?* "Calla still had her bicycle with her," he explained.

He had never been grateful to have a lie at the ready. He *knew* Hammond would make Lucien's business his own.

Hammond looked unconvinced but didn't press the issue.

As he did with his other inspections, Hammond didn't check every single room but a random assortment of them. He didn't ask to see the subterranean ballroom, which provided no small measure of relief to Lucien, but declared he would finish his inspection in the boathouse and greenhouse. "I don't suppose the missing oars ever showed up?" Hammond asked irritably.

"It did not."

"Hmm." But once again, Hammond didn't prod

further. Lucien suspected he would receive an invoice for the oars in the post when he returned.

After sticking his head into Lucien's bedroom and noting the unmade bed with the same "hmm," Hammond announced his walkthrough was complete. Lucien brought him back to the front door.

"Is everything to your satisfaction, then?" Lucien asked. "Will the Greaves family be pleased with the state of the house?"

"The Greaves family can't be bothered to bring themselves back here for any length of time," Hammond answered. "It's all left to my satisfaction." He sighed irritably. "Aside from the oars, everything looks as it should. I'll check the exterior and the outbuildings, and then I'll be on my way."

"Thank you for your hospitality during my visit," Lucien said. He hoped he sounded more sincere than he felt. "I accomplished a great deal of writing." At least that was true. A complete novel, beginning to end. He could hardly wait to turn it in. Peter Fenton would be surprised to see Lucien walk into the offices of Cardwell Press in the space of a day or two, but the editor would be very happy to get that manuscript in his hands.

Hammond nodded, a tight smile on his face.

Lucien opened the door and held it for the caretaker, watching until he turned around the corner of the house, looking at the foundation the entire time. *What a strange man. What a strange village.*

He quickly amended his opinion. *What a strange, horrible village.*

He took one last look at the property's landscaping, bare save for its grass, and the dirt road beyond.

But there was something waiting at the road, about a hundred feet away from the estate. A horseless vehicle.

What the devil?

Without bothering to fetch his coat or hat, Lucien walked out of the house, taking care to make sure Hammond wasn't in the immediate vicinity. He walked to the end of the property's cobblestone lane for a closer look at the steam cab. He could see it clearly now, and it looked just like the one waiting outside the Gull's End inn.

A figure let himself out of the driver's side of the steam cab. Lucien froze, but the figure reached into his coat pocket, and Lucien was quickly able to discern that he was merely smoking.

Was Hammond brought here by the steam cab? If so, why was it parked so far away from the estate?

Lucien quickly answered himself. *Because he didn't want me to see the cab.*

The cab's presence wasn't a coincidence. No one would take the trouble of navigating a coal-powered beast over a rutted dirt road in the middle of nowhere unless he had a very specific reason to.

Or there was a mermaid he needed to re-capture.

He turned around and bolted back to the house, certain Calla was now in danger.

CALLA SAT down at the music stand Lucien used as a desk and picked up a blank sheet of paper and pencil. She hadn't known until now that it was possible to be both nervous and bored.

Her ears strained to hear Lucien open the ballroom door, hear his familiar footsteps descend the staircase. To see his face when he told her he had confirmed their carriage ride to the Manchester airfield and kiss his smile.

Until then, she doodled. Idly, she wrote her name over

and over, first in capital letters, then in lowercase. Sometimes she wrote "Quinn" after it, the only last name she'd ever used. And Lucien had picked it. She liked that.

She drew flowers around the edge of the paper, elaborate blooms she hadn't seen in real life and likely didn't exist. Then she sketched the bowling lane and the ball. She would miss that when they left this place.

Movement caught her attention in the corner of her eye through the opposite glass wall. Something that wasn't the sea lapping at the top of the glass at low tide.

She turned her head and screamed.

A diving-suited figure stood on the seabed, staring at her.

She didn't have to look through the helmet's faceplate to know it was Isadore.

"You *fuck*," she said aloud as if he could hear her. Rage and fear welled up in her, competing for dominance. She rose to her feet and crossed the ballroom. The diving suit didn't move.

Now, she could see more clearly through the glass, see Isadore's smug face through his helmet and the wall.

Calla turned around and ran as fast as her legs could carry her for the staircase. "Lucien!" she screamed, not caring if Hammond was still in the house. "*Lucien!*"

She threw open the door, only to see Lucien running directly for her. "We have to get out of here," he said urgently. "Immediately."

"I know," she said. She pointed to the stairs. "Isadore's down there in a diving suit. I don't know how long it'll take him to get out of the water and get out of his suit, and I don't know if he has help and—"

"He has help," Lucien interrupted. "Hammond brought him here. He's still on the property, but I don't know where."

"How do we escape?" Before he could answer, an idea struck Calla.

It was insane.

But it was the only thing she could think to do, the only way she could give herself an advantage over the man who had tracked her down.

"Watch Isadore," she told Lucien. "He's milling about the seafloor. I have to get something."

Without waiting for his response, she tore off through the house for the bowling room.

She found the ball on the floor, right where they left it before Hammond interrupted their game. She held it against her as she ran back down the corridor to the doorway that led to the ballroom, arms aching, and half-skipped down the stairs.

Lucien, gods love him, was waiting at the foot of the stairs just as she'd asked, staring in horrified fascination at Isadore, who walked the length of the ballroom in the beach's direction. He moved with more speed, more determination than Calla expected from someone in a diving suit.

Which meant he was going to come into the house once he doffed his attire.

Lucien eyed the ball in her hands and immediately understood what she meant to do. "Don't try to talk me out of this," she warned. "He will always come back if I don't kill him."

"I'm not going to talk you out of it," Lucien said. He sounded like he was trying to hold back his emotions, that he was as scared out of his mind as she was, as determined as she was. And she loved him for that. For everything.

"I only have one chance to do this," she said. But before she put her plan, as harebrained as it probably was, into action, she kissed him fiercely.

This will not *be the last time I do that.*

Steeling her courage, she threw the bowling ball at the glass wall. A sickening crunch echoed through the space, and she hefted it at the glass again. This time, she watched in horrified fascination as it smashed the glass. Cracks formed, fatal wounds beyond repair, and water ran in, increasing as the glass weakened. Calla began stripping off her clothes in anticipation of her shifting.

Lucien ran from the stairs as the first rivulets of water leaked into the room. "Get out!" Calla screamed.

"Here," he said, pressing a kitchen knife into her hand.

The ominous groan of thousands, perhaps millions of gallons of seawater against compromised glass sounded, the loudest noise in the world. "Go!" Calla yelled again.

This time, he listened.

He made it up the stairs when before the glass wall gave way, and the sea rushed in.

CHAPTER 14

*L*ucien had to believe that Calla would be all right on her own. *Had* to.

He hated to leave her alone in the ballroom, but he would be of no help in an underwater fight. As he ran through the house to the servants' door in the kitchen, regret ran through him when he thought of the diving suit in the boathouse. It had been there all along while he lived with a mermaid, and he'd never thought to learn to use it.

I don't think a diving suit is something one can learn on his own.

Damn it all, the logical part of him was right.

He had quickly stopped in the kitchen when he realized Hammond was up to something, to pick up a pair of knives on the chance he would have to defend himself. One he left with Calla when he went to the ballroom to warn her, and the other was still in his back trouser pocket. When he stepped outside, he removed it. Knowing his luck, if he didn't, he would fall over and stab himself in the arse.

"Where are you, you bastard?" he said out loud, scanning the scrubby back garden of the property for the caretaker.

Hammond had said he was going to inspect the greenhouse and boathouse. His being in the boathouse made the most sense; Lucien's knowledge of diving suits was quite limited, but someone had to be controlling Isadore's diving suit's air hose bellows.

He threw open the boathouse door, unsurprised to see Hammond waiting on the slip's dock in front of a bellows, pumping air into a hose that snaked off the slip into the water. Lucien briefly flashed back to the last time he was in here, with Calla, and what happened after, but the pleasant memory was quickly wiped away.

A roar rang outside the boathouse, the crash of water rushing against a dam. No, glass.

Please let Calla be all right.

He had to trust that she could take care of herself. "You," Lucien said to Hammond. He held out the kitchen knife in front of him. "What is the meaning of this?"

But Hammond didn't care about him or the weapon. He blanched at the sound of rushing water. "What in God's name was that noise?"

"The subterranean ballroom collapsing in on itself," said Lucien.

"What?" Hammond tried to run for the door, but Lucien pushed him down, putting all of his strength into the blow. The older man fell to the dock, dangerously close to the slip's open water.

Lucien crouched down and held the knife to the caretaker's throat, hoping Hammond didn't notice his hand's fine tremor. Judging by Hammond's bug-eyed stare at the weapon, he didn't.

Lucien never threatened anyone in his life before. He hoped he would never have to do it again.

"You saw her picture in the newspaper, didn't you?" Lucien said. "You saw the reward offered."

"It was one year's wages, and she is an escaped asylum patient," Hammond snapped. He tried to sit up, but Lucien forced him back. He pressed the point of the blade into Hammond's skin, just hard enough to let the prone man know he wasn't in charge.

"She is not. That man who made the offer kidnapped her. He's a criminal."

Hammond tried to sit up once again, causing the blade to deepen its point in his neck just enough to draw blood. Lucien pressed on his chest with his free hand. "Dr. Smythe said she's violent and delusional. I believe him." He coughed under the pressure from Lucien's hand.

There wasn't enough time to berate Hammond for thinking poorly of women who wore trousers. But Lucien was still unsure of what to do next. Push him over the dock into the water, and hope he didn't know how to swim? Was the water even deep enough to be a threat?

Lucien decided to just deliver enough of a blow to his head to make sure he stayed unconscious long enough for him to devise a better plan. But before he could do that, Hammond reared up, heedless of the knife, and crashed his head into Lucien's.

"Fuck!" Lucien yelped. He dropped his knife and staggered to his feet.

Hammond coughed again and didn't rise immediately. Instead, he reached for the discarded knife just as Lucien did.

Lucien kicked it away. The only thing worse than not having a weapon was having one and it being stolen by his opponent. It teetered on the dock's edge.

But Hammond didn't try to get the knife again. He

picked up the bellows and, to Lucien's utter shock, looked like he was going to throw it at him.

"Are you mad?" Lucien couldn't help but ask. Quickly, he reached for the knife and picked it up.

The air hose was wound around the caretaker's wrists, and his arms shook with the machine's weight and his own nerves. "He said a year's wages," Hammond said. "I managed to get him to give me three."

"For God's sake, put that down before you hurt yourself!"

"I don't know why he would give me three years' wages for one odd chit, but I said yes."

"Because he isn't going to give you three years' wages," Lucien snapped. "That man was never going to let you leave this place alive after he took Calla. She's a mermaid."

"No!" snapped Hammond. "There's no such thing. He promised he's a man of his word! He—"

He dropped the machine, fortunately nowhere near Lucien. The dock splintered a little under the bellows' weight, but it was still sound.

The tube wrapped around Hammond's arm sharply tugged at him. Hammond pulled back at it, to no avail.

He was pulled into the water before Lucien could do anything.

CALLA'S SHIFT was nearly violent in its swiftness, the speed with which she did it unsurpassed. She almost wished Lucien could have seen it.

She forced all thoughts of Lucien from her mind to focus on the enemy before her.

Chairs and music stands from the orchestra pit floated by, and she swam through the gigantic hole in the glass wall. She didn't want to give Isadore a chance to step into the ruined ballroom, which would give him easier access to the house itself, in case Lucien had actually listened to her and stayed inside.

I should have told him I loved him before I broke the glass.

Instead, she told him to get away from her and tried not to think of him at all.

She'd managed to keep her grip on the sharp kitchen knife Lucien left her, and she circled Isadore with it in her hand, like a hunter stalking prey.

Finally, *she* was the hunter. It was a heady feeling.

"You fucker," she snarled. Her words caused bubbles to float away from her like they were physically carrying her words through the sea.

Isadore slowly turned around in his diving suit, that eternal smirk on his face. He reached for something behind him, removing a harpoon wrapped in a net that had been strapped to his back, and escaped Calla's notice. Her blood ran cold at the sight; he'd used a similar device to trap her from his submersible. "We aren't done yet," he said. His voice was muffled, but Calla could still hear it, with her ears and through the vibrations carried in the water.

The weapon looked like it was attached to a clockwork-powered propellant, something that could extend its aim. She froze for a second, letting go of the kitchen knife, trying to decide what to do. Isadore wound the weapon's crank, his eyes never leaving her face as she tried to decide what to do.

If she tried to swim away, he could still shoot her with the harpoon.

If she didn't, he was certainly going to capture her again.

If she left, she could be condemning Lucien to a death sentence.

Calla charged, desperate to knock the harpoon out of his hand before he set it off.

Isadore fought back as she expected, but Calla had the advantage of not being bound to the seafloor in a cumbersome diving suit. She was able to force Isadore to keep his arm pointing upward, the harpoon-net away from her. "How did you know I was here?" she asked through gritted teeth. Her voice was muffled by the water that flowed into her lungs, galvanizing her into action.

"You didn't get as far as you thought you did." Isadore's voice was eerily calm, almost flat. He sounded bored, like he was chatting about the weather. "Your navigation senses aren't what they used to be. I didn't learn about them as much as I would have liked to. It was a simple matter of placing an advert in the papers delivered to seaside towns and guessing you still trusted humans enough to hide with them."

Calla's arms ached, both from hauling the bowling ball across the house and fighting for her life. They were starting to shake, and she knew she couldn't hold Isadore at bay much longer.

She spied the hose on the back of his diving suit, delivering life-sustaining air to him, resting on the seafloor. She didn't know where the tube led.

She wasn't going to win the fight over his clockwork weapon. But maybe she could take him by surprise.

She let go of his arm and reached behind him for the hose, yanking on it with all her might, praying she was strong enough to break its seal.

The hose disengaged itself from the diving suit and floated away. Isadore turned his head to see what Calla had done and then grabbed it, frantically pulling a few feet of it towards himself, but it was to no avail.

His horrified face was all the confirmation she needed

to see to know her impromptu plan worked. She knocked the harpoon from his hand and grabbed it before it could float away, aiming it at him.

Isadore barely managed to move a step toward her before his suit filled with water.

She turned away from the sight, unable to watch anymore. Her shaking hands let go of the harpoon, and it floated away to rest on the seafloor.

Lucien paced the length of the dock, peering into the water as he prayed for Hammond to resurface.

The man was cold, strange, and too easily lured by the promise of easy money for Lucien's liking. But he didn't deserve to drown.

And Calla.

Oh, God, Calla. I hope she's all right.

Finally, Lucien could stand it no longer. He grabbed the boat from its wall hook, the same one he used the night he tried to rescue Calla, and a different set of oars, tucking them under his arm. The boat in his hands, he stared at the slip. Should he drop the boat in there?

He glanced at the boathouse's main door that led to the sea. He had no way of opening it.

He would have to do this the same way he did last time. He carried the boat and oars through the pedestrian door and awkwardly ran to the beach with them in hand. He launched the boat as he did last time, noting that it was raining once again, and rowed himself out to the side of the boathouse. "Mr. Hammond?" he shouted.

There was no response.

"Mr. Hammond!" Lucien rowed a few feet away, hoping to catch a glimpse of the caretaker.

Lucien's heart felt like it was going to explode. While he hadn't directly killed a man, his actions contributed to his death, and he thought he might be sick. He'd never been in so much as a schoolyard fight as a boy.

"Calla!" he shouted, his despair echoing across the water.

A dark head rose from the sea. Big, shocked eyes bored into his. "You're all right," Calla said and swam to the boat's side.

"Oh, thank God," said Lucien. He reached for her, pulling her up from the water into a hug as best he could, not caring that his shirt was quickly soaked through. "You're alive."

"Isadore isn't," said Calla into his chest. "I pulled out his air supply hose."

"Hammond was pulled in by the same hose's slack," said Lucien.

"He must be the second dead man in the water right now."

Lucien closed his eyes and swallowed, keeping his nausea at bay. "He couldn't swim," he said somewhat uselessly.

"Neither can you," said Calla, raising a hand to wipe away tears. "So, paddle this back to shore before you capsize again."

Lucien reluctantly let go, and she gracefully slipped back into the water. "I'll meet you at the boathouse," she said. She dove under the water, her tail fluking above the waves.

He rowed back to the beach and carried the boat and oars back to the boathouse. He found Calla on the dock, shifted into her human form. He dropped the boat on the dock, not caring where it landed, and wrapped her in a hug. "I love you," he said. "I should have told you earlier."

"I love you, too," Calla said. Her voice broke. "I don't ever want to leave you. I don't care if we live in a flat in the city and I have to shift in a tub. I want to stay with you forever."

Lucien pressed a kiss to her temple and tightened his hold. "We can go anywhere you want. We can live by the sea."

Calla pulled away just enough so he could see her face. "As long as it isn't Gull's End."

"Oh, God, no. I never want to return to this place."

"Do you think the house is safe to go back to?" she asked. "We have to get your book."

"I'm sure anyone who wanted a subterranean ballroom had the foresight to hire an engineer who would have safe-guards in place for what just transpired," Lucien replied. Arms around each other, they walked along the dock to the door. "Would you like my shirt? I didn't have time to grab my coat."

"What?" For the first time, Calla seemed to see what Lucien was wearing. "You have no coat! And you're soaked!"

"I can be laundered," he said.

"I won't get cold in a little rain," she said. "But you can. Let's get back to the house, and I'll tell you what happened underwater." She paused. "I do hope the rest of it is all right."

"I'm sure it will be," said Lucien. "But we need to get back there before someone comes looking for Hammond and think of a way to explain the property damage."

Calla did something unexpected. She shrugged. "There are two dead bodies down there," she said. "I don't think Isadore can float away so easily in his suit. If anyone asks, he broke the glass, and Mr. Hammond was helping him."

Lucien considered her suggestion. Everything she said was true, except Isadore's smashing into the glass wall. He *had* been looking for Calla; he'd expected to find her in the water, that was all. All they had to tell the authorities and the Greaves family was that Isadore and Hammond caused the damage and drowned themselves in the process.

"All right," he said. "People will definitely ask. Let's use that story."

He laced his fingers through hers, and they ran for the house as the rain picked up speed.

CHAPTER 15

8 November 1887

*D*ear Mr. Quinn,

It is an honor to know an author I've heard of writing a novel in my family's home. I promise I will read one of them someday.

That home you wrote in has been irreparably and gloriously damaged with the destruction of that ridiculous subterranean ballroom my idiot ancestor built. As you were unharmed in the incident, I feel comfortable expressing my glee at being rid of the stupid thing. As no one with a shred of sanity wants the only barrier between the sea and their home to be glass originally forged in the time of Mad King George, the estate was understandably difficult to sell. This is without the added burden of the house being located on the outskirts of Gull's End, the meanest village in England. Repairs are underway, and the house will hopefully be taken off my family's hands sooner than later.

However, the house may now well be haunted by the ghosts of the former caretaker and the fellow found drowned in his diving suit. I cannot say yet if this will be a help or hindrance in finally being rid of the damned property.

If you should feel so inclined, I would love to escort you on a trip aboard my dirigible the next time I visit London. Please be advised that my father and I despise London and travel there very seldom.

Yours sincerely,

Miss Arabella Greaves

P.S.: I realize it would have been better form to cross out the word "damned," but then I would have to re-write this letter so you won't think I made a simple spelling error, and I don't care to do that. I also realize that the best form is to not use the word "damned" at all, but I live aboard a dirigible with my father and you are a man, so there is no need for the use of delicate language.

~

3 January 1888

Dear Mr. Quinn,

I wish you and Mrs. Quinn happiness as you enjoy your holiday season together. While I was surprised to receive a telegram informing me of your irregular marriage ceremony held over Christmas, I am still delighted on your behalf and wish both of you happiness.

I'm pleased with your new book and look forward to putting it out in the world. It will be published on schedule, per our contract.

During our last meeting at the Cardwell Press offices, you mentioned that you intended to write a novel about a village gone mad via supernatural control. I like the idea very much and am eager to read it.

I must say I am surprised by your decision to take to Scotland for the winter, but if traveling to such a cold place will bring you happiness and inspiration, I wish you and Mrs. Quinn well.

Sincerely,

Peter Fenton

Lead Editor, Cardwell Press

~

THE STRONSAY COTTAGE Lucien rented for the winter was warm and snug. It had a bedroom with a lumpy mattress covered in handsewn quilts, a bathroom and kitchen with all the modern amenities, and a small nook he used as a makeshift study. It was also on the edge of a frozen, deserted beach that fed into the North Sea, which Calla was presently emerging from, almost like Venus, as Lucien watched her through the kitchen window.

If Venus had been a mermaid finally getting a chance to swim in the North Sea waters as she dreamed of. Somehow, Lucien doubted the mythical goddess would have enjoyed the cold water.

Calla let herself into the cottage and reached for her favorite towel, hanging on a hook beside the door. "How was your swim?" Lucien asked. He'd prepared tea, and after Calla slipped on her dressing robe, he handed her a cup.

"Refreshing," she replied. She kissed him before taking a sip of her tea. "I like it here."

So did Lucien, but both of them were undecided if they would live in the Orkney Islands permanently. There was a level of privacy here that couldn't be matched anywhere in England, and Calla loved the open water. They had talked about dividing their time between London and Stronsay, but neither were in a rush to make any firm decisions just yet. For now, though, their cottage on the beach was a small, frozen piece of paradise, and he was content to stay for the winter. Or however long Calla wanted to.

She drank her tea in a few quick gulps, then went to the bedroom to dress.

They traveled to Liverpool after finding Isadore's

personal effects, complete with address, in the steam cab he and Hammond rode to Greaves Estate and tracked down the warehouse on the docks where Isadore set up shop. From there, Calla was able to find her way back to the Irish Sea, where she tried to warn her clan about mermaid-hunting humans.

Calla returned three days after she left. Lucien thought they had to have been the longest days of his life until that point. And she returned with the devastating news that her clan refused to listen to her, didn't care about her injuries, and ordered her to leave again. She was disappointed and angry, but she told Lucien she hadn't been surprised at their reaction.

After a short trip to London to meet with his editor and pack, they boarded a dirigible to Edinburgh. But instead of heading directly to the Orkney Islands, the way Calla originally intended, they explored Scotland and were married at Gretna Green after Calla learned about irregular marriages by chance in an inn's dining room.

Calla emerged from the bedroom, wearing her favorite shirt and trousers. She picked up her tea and took a hearty sip. "How is your book coming along?" she asked.

"Just a couple of chapters to go," he replied. "I'm almost finished."

"You'll read it to me, won't you?"

"Are you sure you don't want to?" Her literacy skills had made incredible strides over the preceding months.

She set aside her tea on the table and wrapped her arms around his shoulders. "I'd rather you did it. You find more mistakes that way, and I like to listen to you."

"You distract me when I read aloud," he protested, but it was half-hearted. Calla grinned.

"You love it when I distract you." To prove it, she

lightly nipped at his ear with her teeth, drawing a shudder from him.

"I like those kinds of distractions," he said. "But I love you."

A mischievous glint appeared in her eyes. "Enough to swim with me when the water warms up?"

"Yes," he said.

"You really don't have to swim with me in the North Sea, Lucien," she said.

"As I'm quite poor at it, I don't think I should swim at all," Lucien said. "But I would do it if I could."

"I know," said Calla. "And I love you, too."

They turned to look at the window, at the snowed-over beach and calm stillness of the water, and Lucien knew there was no better place on Earth to be.

ABOUT THE AUTHOR

Jessica Marting is a sci-fi and paranormal romance author, art enthusiast (not quite an artist, despite all that time in art school), an avid reader, and makeup collector. She lives in Toronto.